680320

1997, c52

Thorn

20 —

GHOSTLY

HOOFBEATS

GHOSTLY

HOOFBEATS

NORMAN A. FOX

Thorndike Press • Chivers Press
Thorndike, Maine USA   Bath, Avon, England

This Large Print edition is published by Thorndike Press, USA and by Chivers Press, England.

Published in 1996 in the U.S. by arrangement with Richard C. Fox.

Published in 1997 in the U.K. by arrangement with author's estate.

U.S. Hardcover   0-7862-0807-4 (Western Series Edition)
U.K. Hardcover   0-7451-4980-4 (Chivers Large Print)
U.K. Softcover   0-7451-4981-2 (Camden Large Print)

Thorndike Large Print® Western Series.

The text of this Large Print edition is unabridged.
Other aspects of the book may vary from the original edition.

Set in 16 pt. Bookman Old Style by Al Chase.

Printed in the United States on permanent paper.

British Library Cataloguing in Publication Data available

Library of Congress Cataloging in Publication Data

Fox, Norman A., 1911–1960.
    Ghostly hoofbeats / Norman A. Fox.
        p.   cm.
    ISBN 0-7862-0807-4 (lg. print : hc)
    1. Large type books.   I. Title.
    [PS3511.O968G48 1996]
    813'.54—dc20
                                                    96-26821

For a grand guy in anybody's book,
SULLY SULLIVAN

Chapter One

THE MAN WHO FAILED

Through all the long day he had bucked the hilly country south of Helena, following the ridges and picking the far and seldom used trails; and he got into Montana's capital at dusk, saddle weary and sour minded. He had taken the slant down from Unionville on this last leg of long journeying and so found himself at the head of Main with Last Chance Gulch enfolding him. He saw the lifting magnificence of the Bristol, its lights gay and warm; but he by-passed the hotel for a back-street livery stable and piled down from his horse and had a look around him. He'd never favored the cities, and for a moment he was struck by a remembrance of the Marias country farther north, its wide sky and rough river breaks and vast sweep of dun graze, and was hungry for home. Yet he had the constant, nagging thought that nothing would look the same again, and this in turn reminded him of why he was stopping here. One last chore to do. Everything in proper order — even the admission of defeat.

He gave his horse over to the hostler and came out of the livery and strode along. He was hungry, but going into the Bristol would be like going on parade, and he was in no mood for that. Not tonight. Here, where the gulch pinched together, lived the Chinese, come to burrow in the hillsides and take out what gold the white man had overlooked. They were still doing that, he reflected, though they'd traded pick and pan for other implements. He sought out one of their restaurants, red brick fronted and heavy doored, and got a booth for himself. Chinese food had never struck him as anything to put meat on a man's bones, and tea was a drink for ladies; but he liked the quiet of the place, the unobtrusiveness. One thing about a Chinaman, you never saw any question in his slanted eyes, so you never got to wondering what he was really thinking.

The meal finished, he fished some silver from his pocket and left a good-sized tip. He stacked the coins neatly beside his plate. When he came again to the street, he ambled along, a tall, wide-shouldered, aimless man. A good

many people were abroad, and he wondered if this was a Saturday night. He
put a hand to his lean face and found
it mighty whiskered and decided he was
looking for a barbershop.

He didn't know Helena too well, having visited it only three or four times;
and he couldn't see much sense in
putting a city's main street at the bottom of a gulch, with all the other streets
dipping into it at a slant that would
make a mountain goat leery. The way
the tale was told, they'd struck gold in
this gulch a good many years back, and
the town had sprung up from the old
mining camp, finally getting big and
bold enough to climb out of the gulch
and spread itself across the flats. Probably Flint Manning had walked this very
street in the old days, finding it some
different with the ore wagons rumbling
and the prospectors spreeing. Now that
was something to think about, but
there wasn't any real pleasure in it.
Trouble was, when you wore Flint Manning's boots, you had him at your
shoulder all the time, reminding you of
how high *he'd* stacked.

Night softened the city. Mount
Helena, rearing to the west, had lost its

sharp outline and stood dark and forbidding, a bold mass dwarfing farther hills. Off yonder an N.P. locomotive hooted mournfully, the sound drifting across the valley and dwindling. Somehow it reminded Cole Manning of distance yet to be covered and time running out.

He found a cubbyhole of a barbershop, with the barber shaking out his sheet and a last customer shrugging into his coat and the shine boy dozing in his chair. Manning stepped inside and got into the chair and said, "I'm buying all there is to buy." He sat there, feeling weary in the bones, and gave brief replies as the barber made endless talk while plying shears and razor. The barber, he gathered, didn't hold with Teddy Roosevelt's bolting the party and starting this Bull Moose thing. Well, every man to his own troubles.

He got a haircut and a shave and a hot-towel treatment, and he had the shine boy work on his Justins, not that much could be done after the scuffing those boots had taken down in Bootjack Basin. Talk about a rocky country! He listened to the barber drone on, not half hearing him, all the while studying the collection of shaving-mugs, each inscribed with its owner's name. Politicians, most of them, Manning supposed. State senators and representatives, and the governor, maybe, and some of the bigwigs from Washington, home for the summer. Men like Senator Tom Flowers. Manning craned his neck for a look at the clock and saw that it was nearly ten. Time to be getting up to the senator's house if he was going to make it this evening.

But when he came out of the barbershop, he turned south again toward the Bristol. He'd need a place to bed down, and maybe a room would be hard to come by if he got back late from Flowers's. You couldn't count on sleeping in a livery stable the way you could in a small town. He went into the Bristol and put his name down on the register and was gratified that the clerk didn't so much as raise an eyebrow.

"Keep the key," he told the clerk and didn't bother to go and look at the room. He'd left his bedroll over at the livery stable, so there was nothing to be stowed away.

He walked slowly out of the Bristol, wondering if the clerk would take a second look at his name and come fully awake before he got to the door. But if the clerk didn't, chances were someone would register later and glance back over the names and raise a shout. There was always some yahoo with a memory for the Manning name. And tomorrow morning the reporters would be pounding on his door before he had the sleep pawed out of his eyes. "Just what happened down there in Bootjack Basin, Mr. Manning?" "You get everything tied up in a neat package?" Things like that, with their eyes mocking him.

Now he was into the night again, and he faced himself honestly and knew he'd been postponing the inevitable ever since he'd stepped down from his saddle. He'd taken care of his horse and his hunger, his looks and his bed. He'd frittered away all the time possible, and now there was nothing left but to go and stand up to Tom Flowers and tell the truth.

He gave his belt a hitch; he supposed he should have left his gun hanging over his saddle horn. He called on memory; he had visited Flowers's house once before, and it wasn't hard to find your way around a big town if you worked it the way you did on the range, just remembering the landmarks and not getting your directions tangled. He turned up the slant of State Street and climbed slowly out of the gulch. The slope put an ache in his ankles and got him puffing. Then he headed eastward in the direction of the capitol building, its dome plain to see against the star-shine.

The distance was farther than he'd remembered, and he guessed he should have hired a hack. He counted off the blocks; when he'd put enough behind, he started looking for the big brick house with all the fancy gingerbread on it. There it stood, light shining from the windows. He took the steps up to the porch, and only then did he really face his decision, knowing that what would be said beyond the door could never be unsaid. He slipped his hand inside his shirt and fingered the shield-shaped United States deputy marshal's badge pinned there, thinking of the law it represented and the limitations of the law, thinking of the things that were bigger than the law could ever be.

He had this long, bleak moment, and

in it the shadowy porch seemed peopled with ghostly faces and alive with ghostly voices; but when he tried to harken, they faded out. He was tired, he guessed, more tired than he knew. Then, resolutely, he lifted the iron knocker and let it fall.

The senator himself came to the door and made a blocky shape, peering hard and puckering his silvery brows. "Oh, it's you, Manning," he said. "Come in, boy. Come in."

You couldn't ask for a warmer welcome than that, yet it seemed to Manning that there was something forced in the senator's voice.

He let himself be ushered into the elaborate living room with its garish wallpaper — flowers running every which direction — its fancy furniture, its sputtering gaselier. He felt awkward in this room; his hips threatened the bric-a-brac as he crossed, and his hands fumbled with his sombrero until the senator took it and put it on a marble-topped table that held enough magazines to keep a bunkhouse in reading a whole winter. The senator had a heap of house.

Flowers moved at once to the side-

14

board and said, "Some sherry? But you'd be a whisky man, of course." He turned his back and busied himself with the bottles, making a great clatter. "I thought you'd telegraph from Mannington. Or was your first case too hot for the wires? You wound it up, I reckon, or you wouldn't be here."

Flowers's taste ran to gray business suits and carnations in his buttonhole, but once he'd eaten the dust of the drag, and the mark of earlier years was still upon him. Eastern tailoring couldn't hide the bow of his legs, and Washington life hadn't taken the alkali from his tongue. His face was round and smooth and cherubic, but his eyes had a cattleman's squint. Cole Manning got the uncomfortable feeling that Tom Flowers was looking beyond him to the timbered slopes of Bootjack Basin and the things that had happened there.

He took the drink Flowers proffered and dropped into a big leather chair and stretched out his legs and studied the toes of his boots. That shine boy had done pretty well, considering how little he'd had to work with. He looked at the drink and guessed it was whisky and soda. He'd have preferred a straight shot to one watered down. Same difference as between a stallion and a gelding. He lifted the glass.

The senator did likewise. "Here's to the memory of Flint Manning, God rest him," he said. "Do you know, you favor Flint a lot. Same big-beaked face and smoky eyes. Same loose and ready way of carrying yourself."

Very carefully Cole Manning set his glass on the marble-topped table, and just as carefully he unpinned the badge and laid it down. Gaslight gave to the badge a dull-yellow sheen. "I'm grateful to you for getting me appointed marshal," Manning said. "But I'm resigning. You see, Senator, people were right when they figured I wasn't big enough to fill Flint Manning's boots. I failed down there in the Bootjack."

"Failed!" Flowers ejaculated.

Manning's lips thinned. "Are you surprised? Admit the truth, Senator! You pulled the wires when I asked you for the appointment, but you had your doubts, didn't you? Just like the newspapers; they thought it quite a joke for the son of an old peace officer to try tracking the one lawbreaker who'd escaped Flint Manning. It made good copy, I reckon, all that stuff about a phantom holdup man who struck once and got swallowed by the earth. But it made a pretty tough job."

Flowers put his drink on the sideboard. "Look, son, Flint Manning cast a mighty broad shadow in his day."

Manning said, "Do you think you have to tell *me?* I'm twenty-eight years old, Senator. All my life I've walked in that shadow."

"I see," Flowers said slowly. "And all the while you've wanted to throw your own shadow. It shows on you now, the way the need has twisted at you. Maybe I did you no real favor when I got you that badge."

"Well," Manning said, "you've got it back."

Flowers picked a cigar from the sideboard and absently gnawed the end from it. His round face, schooled by bunkhouse poker and the greater game he'd played since turning politician, showed nothing.

"It would have been a natural, that case you took," he mused. "I can see the newspaper headlines. 'Flint Manning's Son Solves Case That Baffled Famous Father.' But I reckon you didn't have much to go on. Let's see, it was twenty-four years ago when your father was sheriff down there at Mannington and that stagecoach was looted. The mail and a Wells Fargo shipment of currency and jewelry were lifted from the boot. Stop me if I've got any of the facts wrong. I was ranching in the Bootjack at the time, but I'm a little hazy on the details. The money was a payroll for a mining syndicate across the line in Idaho, if I remember right." He sighed. "Imagine that old case stirring to life again. Well, it was just plain luck."

"Luck comes two ways," Manning said. "Good and bad. I've told you I failed."

"I wonder," Flowers said. He restored the unlighted cigar to the sideboard and took a sip of his drink. Then he fell to pacing, limping as he went. There was an ancient bullet wound in his leg, Manning remembered, and a heap of legends as to how Tom Flowers had come by it. Some said Indians; some said rustlers. Others spoke of San Juan and the Rough Riders. Flowers ceased his pacing and shook his head. "Maybe I savvy; maybe I don't," he said. "If

18

you're hell-bent on resigning, I can't stop you, boy. But, off the record, I'd like to know what happened to you in the Bootjack. Do you mind telling me?"

Manning shrugged. "That's why I'm here. I owe you that much."

Yet he knew now why he'd hesitated out there on the porch; and with the sparring done, he still quailed at putting himself at another man's mercy, awaiting his pity or his contempt. He had to ask himself how well he knew Tom Flowers, really. There was Senator Flowers the politician, full of fine speeches and given to back-slapping and glad-handing and slobbering over babies, but there was the ex-cowman, too, the salty one who'd braved the old trails and battled the blizzards and known Flint Manning and Flint Manning's day. One of those two men who were Tom Flowers would understand; the other one might not. That was the size of it.

Flowers said, "Just a minute," and limped over to the fireplace and put a match to the heaped wood. "Had my man get this ready before he took off for the night," he said over his shoulder. "You can have Washington, magnolia blossoms and all. One thing about Montana, no matter how hot it gets by day, it always cools off at night." He watched the blaze catch and fanned it with the bellows. Then he faced about, clasping his hands behind his back and showing a kindly smile. "Well, son?" he said.

Manning picked up his neglected drink and took a good, strong pull at it. Not too bad. Better than drinking alkali water from a hoofprint at that! The liquor warmed his belly and loosened his tongue.

"Most of what happened down there I was in on. The rest I have to guess about," he said. "At the time I asked you for the badge, I had only Sheriff Burke Griffin's report to the papers to go on. He'd arrested some queer old galoot in the Bootjack country named Packrat Purdy. Packrat had a habit of toting home anything that wasn't nailed down. First place Griffin always looked for anything stolen was in Purdy's shack. When somebody's saddle turned up missing a month or so ago, Sheriff Griffin went poking around Purdy's place just as a matter of course. He found the saddle, all right — and that wasn't all. He likewise found the jewelry that was stolen in that twenty-four-year-old robbery. There wasn't any sign of the currency or the mail, but it was the same jewelry, sure enough."

Flowers grinned. "I remember Packrat; he was down there in my day. He's touched, but he's not the kind to do armed robbery. A child's brain in a whiskered head, that's Packrat. You can bet your last blue chip he ran across that loot some place and packed it home."

Manning nodded. "That's exactly the way I figured it. So my first chore was to have a talk with Packrat Purdy and start back-trailing from whatever he told me. I planned as carefully as I could. I might have gone to Mannington by train or stagecoach. But suppose Griffin had spread the word that Flint Manning's kid was returning to his father's old town. I thought likely they'd have a brass band out to meet me, even if they had to go to Butte to borrow one. But I was a marshal, not a visiting celebrity. So I eased up to the basin on horseback, and I had my first look at it early one afternoon. There it was, all that wide sweep of country below me. I'd been on the Marias so long I'd almost forgotten the Bootjack. Do you remember how it looks, Senator?"

"Ah, yes," Tom Flowers said, and his was an old man's face softened by the recollection of a brighter land and a better day. "I remember. And I'm listening, son."

Chapter Two

OLD TRAIL, COLD TRAIL

From this rocky crest where he sat his saddle, Cole Manning could see all the spreading panorama of Bootjack Basin, its rolling green broken by the darkness of clustered trees and the sparkling sheen of dancing creeks, its far wall of hills standing pine-stippled and sunlight-patched. Long absence had dimmed his memory, but time had wrought no real change here, he knew. Eden might have looked like this, he guessed, verdant and majestic and lonely; and he was some surprised at the thought, for he was not a Bible-minded man. But the illusion of an untrammeled land was lost when he looked to the south, for there the smoke of Mannington coiled upward, pale and ethereal, and the distant roof tops showed.

He supposed if he squinted real hard he might make out grazing cattle and riders, perhaps; and when he let his gaze rove, he did see signs of life. Near the basin's center and heading northward were a pair of dust clouds that held his eye until he dismissed them as riddles made remote and inexplicable by distance. He crooked a leg around his saddle horn and dreamed upon the basin.

A man got a feeling of being mighty small when he looked at so much country; he got a feeling of being young in an old, old world. Behind the lofty mountains at his back lay Virginia City, where they'd had the Alder Gulch gold rush nearly half a century ago and Montana's history had got its real beginning. Flint Manning had told him about that long ago, making it scary and something to remember, what with vigilantes and road agents and hangings in the night mixed into it. And Ma there, rocking gently and saying, "Now, Flintridge, do you think that's any story for the boy to sleep on?" The first stockmen had come into the Bootjack at the time of Virginia City's heyday, according to Flint. They'd sought something bigger and more lasting than the gold bubble, those cattlemen; so they'd guided their wagons over the mountain trails and down into the Bootjack. Maybe they'd looked first at the basin from this very crest.

And so he dreamed. While the minutes marched and the sun wheeled lower till he had to tip his sombrero against it, he was content to idle here, looking down on the land where he'd been born and spent his early years. This put an edge to a hunger that was not of the belly. This was like a homecoming, yet it was more significant than that. He wore a badge, and here he would be tested to prove whether he was worthy of that badge. Senator Flowers, who'd yanked the strings and got things fixed up pronto, had made that plain without saying so. There was a trail twenty-four years old that had to be found. His job was to cut sign in the manner of Flint Manning.

Manning. There was a name to conjure with, and it was his name, too. Once another Manning had ridden this basin with the law's badge upon his vest, and once — only once — that Manning had failed. Now how the hell had that set with Flint? There'd been no stigma to his failure. Flint Manning had built himself into a legend, and afterward people had pridefully pointed to his one defeat as proof that the legend was human. They'd remembered that Flint Manning had cut his gun-teeth in the Kansas trail towns and known Miles City in its roaring days, and they'd been pleased as punch that he'd brought his bride to the Bootjack and taken the sheriff's badge. They'd read you off the names of the rustlers and holdup men and killers he'd stowed away in stony lonesome. But Cole Manning had no such glorious record to back *him* if he didn't succeed.

No, he was merely a man who was supposed to live up to another's repu-tation. Tom Flowers was expecting him to fail. So were the newspapers that had jeered at his appointment and even run cartoons showing him sitting full-grown on his father's knee like some silly ventriloquist's dummy. Just remember-ing what those newspapers had said was enough to draw his face tight as he sat contemplating the task ahead. Chasing a damn shadow, that's what the job amounted to! Maybe if he cocked his ears hard he could catch the ghostly hoofbeats of a man who'd rid-den at moonrise on a night twenty-four years gone. But when he listened, he heard only the sighing of the wind in the pine tops, the cawing of crows, and a distant stirring in the brush that might be a black bear lumbering along.

Well, there was no use roundsiding here, mooning the time away. He'd put plenty of miles behind him since sunup, but it was still more than a hoot and a holler to Mannington. He dropped his foot to the stirrup, lifted his reins, and began picking a trail down the slope.

To his right a creek bubbled, making a gossipy murmur; and as he descended he got into thicker timber, cottonwood and black birch and quaking aspen, till his view of the basin was shut off and he had the feeling of wending through a leafy tunnel. This was late spring, when all the hills stirred to sudden life and the birds took to nesting again. Overhead an eagle flew in tireless circles; and as Manning rounded a turn of the trail, a ruffed grouse took fright at his coming. A ridiculous bird, putting on its ancient act, pretending it was nigh unto death by flapping its wings and clucking and staggering around like drunk. The whole game was to keep his attention from its chicks, that went rolling out of sight under a bush. Manning had to grin.

Dropping steadily downward, he again came upon a promontory, a rocky ledge that gave him a look into the basin, though he got no such spreading view as he'd had above. He was nearly to the basin's floor, and the afternoon was far gone, and he was reminded that he'd made no noontime stop. He thought of off-saddling and having some hard bread and meat from his saddlebag, and then he saw those dust clouds again. They'd grown with proximity, and their northward sweep had brought them almost below him. And suddenly they got a tight hold on his attention, for something about them now suggested grim pursuit and a desperate effort at escape. This first real scent of trouble wrought a change in him, stiffening him in his saddle.

He was riding his own horse, a sorrel mare he'd fetched from his Marias ranch. He had a lariat at the saddle horn, a Winchester at his right knee, and a pair of field glasses in his saddlebag. Getting the glasses to his eyes, he focused them on the growing dust clouds. The one to the front was stirred by a light spring wagon with two people on its seat. There were trees below, and the wagon vanished into a clump, but it reappeared again. Fiddling with the focusing screw, he made out one of the wagoners to be a little old woman, a shawl about her head, a pair of crutches beside her. The other, driving the team and lashing frantically at it, was apparently a Levi's-clad boy. There they went, bowling along like the devil was at their heels. But as Manning watched, the breeze whipped away the driver's sombrero and long tawny hair bannered out. That overall-clad driver was a girl.

Quickly Manning swung his glasses to the rear, whistling softly. A quarter of a mile behind the wagon came five horsemen hunched over their saddle horns and swinging their quirts hard, a big, black-browed man in the lead. They flashed into timber and out again, the big man still up ahead. This one lifted a gun and fired at the wagon, giving Manning a sudden sense of un-reality, for the man was fetched so close by the glasses, yet the sound was so distant. Manning stowed the glasses away and made a quick decision. Then he was jogging his horse and heading down the slope at breakneck speed.

He might have decided that this affair was none of his, but he was too busy keeping the sorrel from somersaulting in that wild descent. Riders could raise dust down below, where the sun got in a good day's work on the basin's floor, but here on the shadowed slope the ground was still spongy from the spring rains; he'd seen snow patches on the higher levels today. Fresh mud and gumbo now thudded up against his chaps and stirrups, and the horse skidded, almost pitching him over the horn. But still he did not slacken his pace. Impatience made him heedless of danger, and a heady anger grew in him.

Riders who tried gunning down a girl and a crippled old woman needed their manners mended, he told himself. And he was just the gent to take a try at the mending. His desire to see Packrat Purdy was urgent, but this other little chore could be taken care of first. Such was the run of his thoughts as he came sliding and plunging off the slope.

Before him the wagon road cut through a clump of trees perhaps a quarter of a mile away. As he galloped obliquely toward this thicket, a stand of ancient cottonwoods, high and gnarled, he saw the wagon thunder into the trees. Just for a second he had a glimpse of the strained face of the girl as she leaned forward, lashing at the team. She turned her head slightly, and fear stood naked in her face. He wanted to shout, to cry out that he was a friend coming to help; but he knew his voice would be drowned by the clatter of wheel and hoof. Then the wagon was swallowed by the trees.

He spurred hard and neck-reined his horse into the cottonwoods; he drew the mount to a rearing halt. He was panting, and above the beating of his heart he heard the diminishing thunder of the wagon and a rising rataplan of hoofbeats that told him the pursuers were drawing near.

Not much time. Not near enough time.

But now he got the ghost of a notion, and he moved swiftly. Taking his lariat, he nudged the horse across the road and wrapped the rope around the trunk of a tree. Playing out the hemp, he stretched it taut across the wagon road and tied it to another tree opposite at a level to catch a horsebacker high across the chest. He was all thumbs at the job, but he got it done in time.

31

Dismounting, he leaned against the tree; and holding tight to the reins of his horse with his left hand, he waited, his lips quirked with faint smiling.

Now the five were loping into the timber. He saw them shape up, a compact knot of horsemen; and thus bunched together, they hit the rope at full tilt. For a moment there was a tangle of arms and legs, men sprawling grotesquely, shouting their anger and surprise, the horses rearing and plunging. Two of the cayuses bolted along the back trail; and Manning stepped forward, waving his sombrero and letting out a rebel yell that sent the other mounts galloping. One of the spilled riders, down on his hands and knees, tried to snatch at trailing reins. Manning saw him fail in this attempt and have to roll to avoid the horse's flailing hoofs. Moving back a few paces, Manning again put his shoulders to the tree. He got his gun out and held it loosely in his hand.

He said, "Since when did it become open season on girls and old ladies?"

The big, black-browed leader was the first to his feet. He brushed at himself and shook his shoulders like a grizzly about to go rampaging, but shock was still in his eyes. He flexed his arms, and his hand moved toward his holstered gun. He looked at the Colt in Manning's hand and changed his mind.

"How about the rest of you boys?" Manning asked. "Any busted bones? Now shuck your guns and toss them over here. Damn it, do as I say!"

They were picking themselves up, one by one, and they obeyed in sullen silence, their eyes hard-shining and their shoulders stiff. When their weapons lay at Manning's feet, he crouched, put his own gun within quick reach, wrapped the reins loosely around his left arm, and busied himself at jacking the shells from the collection of forty-fives.

Watching him, the big leader said in a voice shaking with anger, "You're making a bad mistake, stranger. No man crosses Mack Torgin and gets away with it. This is one day. Tomorrow's another."

Torgin. Manning looked up at him sharply, seeing a blocky body and a blocky face in which angry arrogance showed. Even if you'd been only eight years old the last time you'd laid eyes on this man, you'd remember him, especially that rumbling voice that started deep in his chest and sounded like thunder in the hills. A tough one, Torgin, with a knock-'em-down-and-drag-'em-out kind of toughness. Some intelligence, too. Enough to make Manning doubly careful.

Yet it was not Mack Torgin who concerned Manning at the moment and filled him with edgy wariness but the man who stood behind Torgin, a slender, hawk-faced man with a pair of eyebrows that were pointed and a widow's peak showing beneath the brim of his shoved-back sombrero. He couldn't remember that one, though the fellow looked to be in his late thirties and might have been around in the old days. He had the bluest pair of eyes Manning had ever seen; they were like glacial ice, and they didn't blink. Snakes looked at you that way. You could discount the other three, an unshaven, shabby trio who seemed to have got a bellyful of rough riding. You could even discount Mack Torgin now that his fangs were drawn. But that icy-eyed one would be dangerous even if you got him tied hand and foot.

The fellow was looking hard at Manning, and he said in a quiet voice, "Mack, let me say a few words to this bucko. Step aside, Mack."

Now a man didn't need clearance to make his voice reach. Manning's gun came rigid in his hand, and he stood erect and tossed away the shells he'd jacked from the guns. They rattled through the leaves of a serviceberry bush and were lost. "Just hold it the way you are," Manning said. "Both of you." He grinned at Torgin. "So it's Mack Torgin, eh? You've put on more beef since I saw you last, but likely you don't remember me. It doesn't matter. What's more important is a little idea I'd like to get across. The next time I see you with a gun aimed at a girl, I'll not stretch a rope. I'll blow you out of your saddle."

Torgin's eyes squinted down. "So we've met before. I'll place you in a minute, mister."

"No," Manning said. "I don't think so."

Icy-Eyes took a slaunchwise stand and said softly, "Oh, hell," moving his right hand to the second button of his shirt. A hide-out gun? A small-caliber job that would be just as effective at a short distance as a forty-five? Before

Manning could stop the play, Torgin said hastily, "No, Gal! Not now! Take my word and don't try it!"

Icy-Eyes — Gal — said, again, softly, "Oh, hell," but he let his hand fall.

Manning said, "Thank your boss, Gal. He just saved your life."

Torgin still peered at Manning; Torgin's lips worked, but the words didn't come. He was violence held in check by the thinnest of tethers. He stared on through the timber where the wagon road wended, then looked back at Manning. "You've given those two enough head start that nobody will ever catch them," Torgin said. "From here on, the timber gets thicker, and there are coulees and canyons where they could hide from an army. You'll answer to the law for this, stranger."

Manning thought of the badge he could reveal by a flick of his vest, but he only grinned. "Don't try passing yourself off as a posse, Torgin. Burke Griffin is still the law in the Bootjack."

"You seem damn well acquainted," Torgin snapped, and his anger overwhelmed him. "A jail breaker is fodder for any honest man's guns, mister. You didn't want to see an old woman stopping lead, eh? Well, that 'old woman' happened to be a fugitive in disguise. That was Packrat Purdy, who busted out of the Mannington jail today. And we'd have corralled him if you hadn't horned in, damn you!"

Manning gestured with his gun. "Start walking," he said tonelessly. "All of you. If you hurry along, maybe you'll catch up with your horses. Do you hear me? Get going!"

Gal showed him a sardonic twist of the lips. He was a cool one, Gal, not fussed by all this, and he looked Manning over like he was memorizing him. He was slow about this, and bold and thorough and altogether deadly. "We'll meet again, feller," he said. "That's a promise."

He turned then; and Torgin, giving Manning another hard stare, turned with him; and the five began marching back over the wagon road, heading south. Manning held his gun as long as they were in sight, and even afterward he was taut and wary, mindful that they might come skulking back. But if he had been angry on the slant down into the basin, he was angrier now, but for a different reason. Damned if he hadn't been dealt a bad one!

Packrat Purdy had been in that wagon. Purdy had escaped; and he, Cole Manning, had unwittingly helped make good his escape. That was the size of it. And Purdy was the one man who might have given him a clue to the identity of the holdup man he sought. Once there'd been a trail, faded and dimmed by the passing years. Now that trail had grown even dimmer.

Casing his gun, he reached up and unfastened his lariat and slowly began coiling it. He'd given Torgin's bunch a mighty rough go with that rope, but he'd tripped himself as well. He fastened the rope to his saddle horn and stepped up to leather and was a thwarted man, bitter with his own thinking.

Chapter Three

QUESTING GUNS

To the north the country turned wild and tangled, and here Manning rode in spite of Torgin's saying that no one could overtake that wagon now that it had a head start. He soon saw what Torgin had meant, but still he tried cutting sign, finding this most futile of efforts less futile than doing nothing. Here the timber was thicker, almost impenetrable in places, and the flat floor of the basin was scarred with draws and ridges. The hills began to pinch in closer, canyons fingering back into them and cliffs of rose-colored rock upthrusting. Creeks, fed by small springs and the melting snow of the high peaks, spilled downward, gurgling and splashing across the game trails, and the wagon road had long since petered out to nothing.

At first it had been easy to track the wagon, but with the terrain turning rockier, all sign faded. Scrubby timber masked angling coulees, and he might have passed within shouting distance of a hidden wagon without seeing it. Purdy hadn't had much of a start, but it had been enough.

Still, a man couldn't quit just because the going had got hard. He got to thinking that no part of his experience had fitted him for this work until it dawned on him that this was like hunting strays on his home range up north. You followed sign while you had it to follow, and when all else failed, you just kept looking. And sometimes when you were about to turn back home, empty-handed and hungry in the gut, you caught a flicker of brown off yonder and found your strays. But while he made today's search, Manning was also keeping a careful eye on the back trail. Torgin's bunch might be back into saddles and making a search of their own. They'd had blood in their eye, that outfit.

He'd remembered Torgin, even though Torgin hadn't recognized him, which was natural enough. Cole Manning had been a child when he'd left Bootjack Basin, while Torgin, pushing fifty now, had been a man even then. Manning remembered him as a big voice on a town's street and a big hulk in a saddle.

Torgin's Slash 7 spread lay to the south, tucked into the west wall of the basin this side of Mannington, and there'd been whispers in the old days that a wide loop and a running iron had built it. Manning judged that the years hadn't softened Mack Torgin, but it was the man called Gal who really stuck in his mind. He could still feel those icy-blue eyes on him and hear that soft voice. He shook his head to rid himself of the memory.

Now why the hell had Torgin, of all people, taken on the chore of running down a jail breaker?

That gave Manning something to chew on, but he put only part of his mind to the task. He was still looking for sign and getting a lost feeling out of such a cluttered land. No ranches up here, as far as he remembered, but he couldn't be sure. He didn't know these odd corners of the basin, though he recalled riding behind his father's saddle long ago. Let's see, he'd been four when that phantom holdup man had struck, and eight when Flint Manning had decided to give up sheriffing and move out of the Bootjack to try his hand at ranching along the Marias. Likely

41

much of what seemed like remembrances from this basin had really come
from tales told by his father later.
Things like his knowing today how
Mack Torgin was rumored to have got
his start.

Now that he studied on it, it came to
him that he'd known his father for just
exactly half his life. He'd been fourteen
when that talk of licking Spain had
filled the air and Flint Manning had
gone down to Butte and signed up with
the Third United States Volunteer Cav-
alry. Hard riding men they'd wanted,
who knew how to handle a gun. Men to
make up the Montana Squadron. Flint
Manning needn't have gone — he had
a wife and a kid and a ranch to care
for. But President McKinley had called
for five hundred volunteers out of Montana and got nearly three times that
many when you counted in the infantry
belonging to the Montana National
Guard.

Yes, Flint Manning had gone to the
war and got no farther than Camp
Thomas, where the Montana men had
waited a month for uniforms and horses
and carbines and made bold, brave talk
of serving in Cuba, while their clothes

turned to tatters and some men went barefooted. Rainy weather had come to Georgia, and the fever had got Flint Manning. You could find his name on the roster — Sergeant Flintridge Manning, former occupation — cowboy. Most of old Troop L had been cowboys, though you could also find laundrymen and civil engineers and carpenters and what not on the list. The rest of them had still been roundsiding in Georgia when the Spaniards had called it quits; it was Montana's infantry that had died in queer-sounding places like Malate and Caloocan and La Loma and Cavite in the Philippines.

Well, they'd sent Flint Manning home in a flag-draped box, and Flint Manning's wife had been mighty brave about it, and mighty proud; though now that Cole Manning looked back on it, he guessed his mother had died then, too, though she'd lived till he was twenty and had got the Marias spread built up to something a man could be chesty about. It was like she'd held on hard till she'd got him raised. A lot of folks had helped. They'd do anything for Flint Manning's boy, but the hell of it was that they always acted like they expected him to measure up to Flint, and that made anything he did not quite good enough. A man got tired of that. Mighty tired.

He'd got his mind back around to the old bitterness that had brought him here to the Bootjack, and he pushed such thinking aside, needing a clear head as well as a clear eye. If he had to hark up the ghost of Flint Manning today, it should be to help, not hinder. He was still looking for sign when suddenly a shot brought him to instant alertness.

He was nearly to the north end of the basin and had got into a stretch of comparatively open country with the hills looming by and here and there a tree clump. When he felt the airlash of a bullet as the gun sounded again, he came out of the saddle fast, but he tossed the reins over his horse's head to keep the sorrel ground-anchored. That was instinct. He hit the ground and felt the bite of gravel. He got on his hands and knees and went scrambling into a cluster of rocks, his ears tuned for another shot and the cold knowledge in him that you never heard the one that killed you. He got into the rocks, and here, sheltered, he peered out, seeking the gunman.

Over yonder in the trees, he decided. Torgin's bunch? He raised himself, letting his Stetson show, and again the gun spoke, the bullet striking the rocks and ricocheting, the whine harsh in his ears. But this time he'd marked the telltale wisp of smoke. Not from the trees but from the top of a cutbank farther to the right. One person was shooting, using a hand gun at that. Gal? There'd be persistence in that fellow.

A smoky anger began growing in Manning. He looked out to where his horse stood patiently anchored; the mare seemed an eternity away. He could whistle up the mount, but as soon as he lifted himself to the saddle, he would be exposed, and that gun would speak again. He looked about him; the terrain had become very important now. Yonder cutbank was at the foot of a slope where the timber rose in dark ranks. Between the cutbank and this rock pile was the tree clump where he'd first supposed the bushwhacker to be. To the rear of his present position was a stand of lodgepole pine, thick and high.

Overhead the open sky mocked him.

He made his study carefully. He could maneuver back to the pines by keeping the rock cluster between him and that questing gun. This he did, moving slowly; and he was sweating hard and his hands and knees were sore by the time he gained the woods. Into the timber and sure that he was screened from view, he stood erect and had a careful look toward that cutbank. He glimpsed slight movement up there but could make no identification. One person, he judged.

Now he could whistle his horse over and, mounted, burrow deeper into the woods and so put the safety of distance between himself and the gun slinger. He started to raise his fingers to his lips, but his anger had grown, and he began calculating again. These woods swept in a semicircle to the north and west, almost to the edge of the cutbank. If he was careful, he could get behind the bushwhacker.

He began moving through the trees, hurrying as fast as he dared but being heedful not to make a great noise. He took a good half hour at this, picking his way around deadfalls and worming through bushes, and the sun was tipping the crest of the hills when he ventured out of the timber at the foot of the cutbank. He was directly below the gun slinger unless that person had gone maneuvering, too.

Now he must chance openness, and he drew in a long, hard breath. Taking a look at the loads of his gun, he soft-stepped around the embankment and began climbing. The muscles of his back ached with expectation of a bullet; he was sure he was making enough noise to rouse echoes, but he got to the top unchallenged and then he saw her.

It was the girl again, the one who'd driven the wagon for a disguised Packrat Purdy. He was sure of that. She lay flattened out on the edge of the cutbank, a forty-five ponderous in her hand and all her attention riveted on that rock pile down yonder. He was reminded of a dog that had treed a squirrel and was waiting patiently at the bottom of the tree, certain that his quarry must be where last seen. He was grinning as he set one foot cautiously ahead of the other until he was almost upon her. Then he said sharply, "Hey, you!"

She rolled over and propped herself on her left elbow, completely startled, and he had his first clear look at her. She was about twenty, he judged. She wore a plaid shirt and a pair of faded Levi's, and her hair, taffy-colored and loosened when she'd lost her sombrero on that wild wagon ride, tumbled about her shoulders. In spite of the scare that showed, her face was pretty. She looked at him wide-eyed and speechless, and then she brought up her gun.

She was going to shoot, no fooling about it. He had a quick remembrance of her fright when he'd cut down the slant a couple of hours before and almost intercepted her wagon. She'd thought him one of her pursuers then, and she thought so now. He plunged forward headlong, hurling himself upon her. The gun roared, the flash almost blinding him, and he'd have sworn that she'd scorched his eyebrows. His fingers frantically sought her right wrist; he found it and twisted hard. She released the gun, but she wrapped her arms around him, rolling him over. She was surprisingly wiry, and he felt her fingernails and teeth. He was panting by the time he got her pinned down and straddled her, his hands hard against her arms. She glared up at him, angry and scared and defiant.

"Going to behave?" he demanded.

"Let me up!"

He shook his head. "Only if you'll be a good girl. Where's Packrat Purdy?"

"Where you'll never find him!"

He thought of the badge he might display and decided against it. "Look," he argued, "you've got me pegged wrong. Unless you're a stranger in the basin, you must know Torgin's crew by sight. I'm not one of them."

She squirmed, trying to release herself. "You're that new one, the fellow who never shows in town."

"Not me."

"I saw you try to head off the wagon!"

He glanced aside and saw her gun lying just out of reach. He could get up real quick and kick that gun over the edge of the embankment and hand her a cuff if she came at him with claws and teeth again. You couldn't get anywhere sitting on a lady's brisket making small talk, that was sure.

He took his hands off her and was levering himself upward when a gun spoke again. A distant gun. This time he felt the lead tug at his sombrero, and he instantly flung himself aside and went rolling. He had a blurred glimpse of sky and timbered slope and judged that this second questing gun was high in the timber. Now who the hell was buying in?

The girl was up at once and running. He tried to snatch at her ankle as she passed, but she moved too fast for him. She flung herself over the edge of the embankment, and he lurched to a stand, heedless of anything. That hidden gun spoke, the hills echoing the shot. Dirt spurted at Manning's feet, but it was anger that blinded him. He'd been so near to Packrat Purdy once again, and now this chance was slipping away. He looked over the rim of the embankment. The pitch wasn't steep, and he saw the girl roll to a stop below. She picked herself up and darted into the timber from which he had so lately emerged. The gun spoke again, the dirt lifting even closer. Manning flattened himself and rolled over the lip of the cutbank.

When he'd got to the bottom, the girl had disappeared. He wasn't worrying about her, not at the moment; she'd left her gun up above, so she was no real menace. But who was shooting from the timbered slope? Torgin? Gal? Why should either of them interfere between him and the girl? Packrat Purdy? Was Purdy up there covering the girl's back while she'd hunkered below at a more advantageous point, ready to discourage any pursuit?

That made a lot more sense. And that left his work cut out for him. He edged around the bottom of the cutbank and took a careful look up the slope. A considerable swath of slanted openness lay between him and the first of the timber, and he glanced about to see how best he could reach that timber. No sheltered way was apparent. But suddenly he was done with pussy-footing, and he darted out. Bending low, he ran a zig-zagging course upward toward the timber, expecting any moment to hear the gun speak.

He was panting hard and perspiring again when he got into the trees. Here he paused and listened. Only the small sounds of the woods reached him; some unseen rodent rattled its claws against rock; birds made their tiny noises in the trees. A disturbed world had restored itself.

But still he climbed, moving Indian-fashion, ready to dodge behind a tree if need be. Wild currant bushes grew here, and he moved among these as silently as he could, seeking, always seeking, his nerves growing raw with the quest. He began to itch in a dozen places. Often he turned and looked below. From the basin's floor the timber had seemed unbroken; yet wherever that second gun slinger had stood, he'd had a clear view of the top of the cutbank. And then Manning came into an open place and could look down to where he'd tussled with the girl, and thus he knew that he'd found the spot.

There was other evidence as well, ample evidence. No one was here, but on the ground a couple of empty shells glinted in the last sunlight. He bent and examined these. Forty-fives. He cocked his head and keened the silence, his own gun ready. A hawk wheeled lazily overhead. Manning let the empty shells drop and looked about and saw where the man had stood, for the bootprints were mighty plain in the damper earth of the slope. He shook his head in puzzlement. A big man had left those prints; and Purdy, from the glimpse he'd got of the fellow, had been small enough to pass for a woman.

He dropped to hands and knees and studied those tracks intently, wanting to know all they could tell him. The toes were turned in slightly. The heels were run over; and the sole of the left boot was worn, leaving in the center of the print a mark like a jagged star. That was something to remember. Again he thought of Torgin and Gal. And still that notion made no sense.

It was getting on to dark, and there wouldn't be much twilight once the sun dropped behind the hills. He looked about farther and saw that the prints led away from this clearing and on up the slope. Had the one who'd sided the girl gone circling to join her? Or, having saved her from a tight, had the fellow lost all further interest? There was no telling.

And then, because there was nothing else to do, Manning came back down the slope to the openness below and trudged across it toward his horse. Anger still smoldered in him, and his disappointment grew with the gathering shadows. As well look for a single pine cone in a forest as to try any further tracking tonight. The girl had got away from him, and so had the man who'd bought into this business. Any way you added it up, the day totaled zero.

He wondered if he could reach Mannington tonight and judged that he'd better bed down instead. Pretty late now for long riding.

Yet after he'd got aboard his horse and ridden southward till he found a camp site with trees and water, he still thought of Mannington and a last hope that lay there. Possibly Purdy had talked before his escape. Possibly Sheriff Burke Griffin had wrung some information out of the old eccentric and thus discovered how Packrat had come by that long-missing loot. Perhaps Purdy had even named a name and thereby unmasked that phantom rider whose hoofbeats now echoed across the years. There was that one crumb of hope, and he held to it hard.

Chapter Four

AT SLASH 7—

A sullen anger in him, Mack Torgin tramped along with his men strewed out behind and Gal a silent one at his right elbow. They were wearing guns again, for Torgin had sent two of his crew back to the cottonwood clump to get the weapons, and these men had returned with word that the stranger had vanished. This had both worried Torgin and whetted his wrath. And now they had worked far south of that clump of trees where the stranger had spilled them, and Torgin's boots were beginning to pinch. A big-footed man who had his boots handmade, it was his particular vanity to take a size smaller than comfort called for. In the saddle he never suffered from this, but now he was limping. He sat down heavily on a rock and lifted his neckerchief and wiped his broad forehead.

"Damn him!" he said explosively.

His men came to a stop, standing listlessly and looking tired. None of them spoke, and this increased Torgin's irritation. They'd tasted his temper before, he knew, and he'd got them trained to walk soft and talk soft when he was in a mood; but they didn't have to stand around like so many stumps. Trouble with these thirty-a-month boys was that they didn't have any more sense than the cattle they herded. Not a lick more! Give them a dollar or two to jingle in their pockets and a slug of whisky to warm their bellies and they were as faithful as any Fido, but you had to do all their thinking for them.

He looked up at them morosely. "Well, are you going ahead and see if you can catch those broomtails? Or do I have to boot you down the trail?"

Three of them at once moved on. But Gal stood. His blue eyes stayed unblinking, and when he spoke his voice was as soft as ever. He said, "If you'd only stepped aside, Mack. I could have got my sneak gun out and pinned him against that tree like he was nailed there. But I couldn't make any play with you standing in the way."

Torgin showed him a twisted grin. "You've come to love me a lot in a mighty short time."

Gal shook his head. "Don't fool yourself, Mack, on one count or the other. I had nothing against that galoot but the shaking up he gave me, and long ago I quit hunting trouble for trouble's sake. As for you, you're my bread and beans around these parts. I'm not forgetting that. As long as I work for you, I'll trouble them that trouble you. But you spoiled my chance back there. I want to know why."

Torgin's black brows pulled together. "I wish I could tell you, Gal. Some things a man has a chance to figger out in advance; some come to him like a whisper in the ear. We were playing it risky as it was. Purdy's a jail buster, but I reckon it wouldn't have set well with basin folks if he'd stopped one of our bullets. And there'd been hell to pay for sure if we'd tagged Laura. You can savvy that. This stranger might have been another matter. Probably no one would have taken up for him. But I just couldn't be sure."

Gal nodded, his lean face thoughtful. "You were playing a hunch, then?"

"More than that. I've seen that hairpin before. But where? Miles City — Helena — frolicking in Butte? Maybe at some rodeo. Or in the stockyards at Chicago.

Here's the question. Is he just a drifter who bought in because he saw a girl getting chased? Or is he something more than that? I want to know before we use the meat ax on him."

His lips quirking slightly, Gal asked, "Do you always play it so safe?"

Torgin looked up and gave him that twisted grin again. "I've never served any stretch in stony lonesome."

Gal shrugged. "It gives you patience," he said. "But it likewise teaches you to grab a chance when it's right in front of your nose."

"Like the time you broke out?"

"For instance."

"Times change," Torgin said. "Nobody plays as rough as they used to twenty years ago. You'll find that out when it gets safe enough for you to stir around a bit."

"What's next, then?" Gal asked.

But Torgin scarcely heard him, for he was lost in thought. Damn a face that had no name you could tie to it, that brought no remembrance of where you'd seen it before! It was like something floating out yonder, just beyond your finger tips. You started groping back across the years, seeking out the

58

lost ones, remembering a man who'd bought you a drink in some far saloon, or one who'd asked you for the makings on a distant trail. You grasped at some fragment of memory and thought for a minute that you had it in your hand, and then it was gone. And the more important it got to you, the harder it was to reach.

"It'll come back," he said aloud. "I'll place him sooner or later."

On down the trail, someone raised a shout. Gal looked in that direction and said, "They've spotted the horses," and started walking that way.

Torgin rose from the rock and limped after him, cursing again. Roundsiding for a few minutes hadn't made his boots any more comfortable. He came out of scattered timber to catch a glimpse of his four men and the missing horses. Those cayuses had fallen to grazing, and the men were spreading out, trying to surround them. The men moved as carefully as though walking on thin ice. But the horses were already showing signs of skittishness, as if maybe they were getting ready to head back to the wild bunch. Torgin wanted to shout, but he fought down the impulse, knowing it would booger the beasts.

Trouble was, he'd got his saddle stock by combing the mountains for those ugly, short-legged little cayuses, and even though they were inbred and stubborn and mean, they broke to saddle after a fashion. But you couldn't depend on them any more than the weather. You thought you had them trained, but when you needed one bad, you had a wild horse on your hands. Like now.

Gal's own mount, stocky and ungraceful of body, tossed its head, snorted, and took off. One of Torgin's men who'd maneuvered around behind the animal threw up his arms, waved his sombrero, and turned the horse. It ran blindly toward Gal. He stepped aside, nimble as a kootch dancer in a Butte honky-tonk, and snatched at the reins as the mount went by. Then he was up, not using the stirrups but hitting the leather Pony Express style. Torgin let out a ragged breath. A fine figure in the saddle, Gal. Long-limbed and graceful and part of the horse. He was at once shaking out a noose, and with the other horses bolting every which way, he settled that noose over the head of Torgin's mount. He led the beast up.

"Thanks!" Torgin grunted and lifted himself to the leather. He settled himself comfortably and sighed. Damn but it was good to get off his feet!

That Slash 7 hand who'd maneuvered the farthest around the horses had caught up a bolting mount. Now he was trying to turn the other two fugitives back. They were showing a flurry of hoofs and manes, and one cayuse slipped past him. He herded the other toward the men, who moved in fast to catch it. Torgin saw the two hands hold a gesticulating conference out there in the openness. They ended up by both climbing aboard the cayuse. The mount showed its resentment at the double load by bucking hard for a few minutes, but the two men stuck, the one clinging grimly to the other, and the session ended with the cayuse doing some spiritless crowhopping. Torgin and Gal jigged their mounts forward, and the four horses became a compact bunch.

Torgin peered to the south. "That other jughead is loping toward home," he said with satisfaction.

Gal looked back toward the north, his face showing a question but no great interest. He was a remote spirit and at the same time a ready one.

Torgin shook his head. "It's getting on toward dark. We wouldn't find a thing, Gal. Not a thing. We'll go home for the night."

And so they rode along, no words between them and only the creak of saddle leather, the jingle of bit chains breaking the silence. They skirted the western wall of the basin with the shadows sliding down the slopes and all the land turning soft and purple and shapeless. In the last of the light, someone said unnecessarily, "Here's the canyon." They dipped down a steep, narrow trail and saw the ranch buildings a few hundred feet below them, a scatteration of frame and log. Sounds rose distinctly in the clear mountain air — a door creaking on rusty hinges, a man calling across the yard, a dog barking.

Light showed below in the bunkhouse, and someone said, "The rest of the crew's back."

The descent made, Torgin swung down before the house, handing over his reins to one of the men. He glanced toward the corral and saw the missing cayuse standing at the gate, looking

frisky and sure of itself. A taste of the blacksnake was what the jughead needed! Some calves were penned in another corral, not bawling their fool heads off but standing in a droopy fashion like they didn't have enough legs under them. It was getting too dark to count from this distance, but Torgin judged there were more calves than there'd been this morning, and this angered him. Damn the sick ones that had to be fetched in! They brought him a sharp remembrance of a scheme gone wrong, and he was a sour man on his own doorstep.

The house was frame and two-storied and needed paint and was graced with no such unessential fooforaw as a porch. He groped his way inside and slung his hat onto the parlor table. He could use a fire, with the evening chill coming down, but he was in no mood for the labor of making one. He got a kerosene lamp burning, adjusted the wick, and found a bottle he'd stashed in the fireplace woodpile. Dropping down into a rawhide-bottomed rocker, he stretched out his legs and set his teeth to the cork of the bottle. It would be nice to get those boots off, but he wasn't up to the tussle.

A pull at the whisky warmed him and took some of the edge off the disappointments of the day. Still, he felt no more kindly toward that drifter. Now where had he seen that face before? Lean and dark, the cheekbones high enough to be an Indian's. Hazel eyes and a mouth that was pleasant enough but could shape up mean. He pondered on this and again gave up the speculation. The answer would come to him in the middle of a night or in a day's riding, while his mind was on something else. Right now he'd better be thinking about his next move. That was the ticket. He'd had a pretty big stake in Packrat Purdy, and Purdy had got away from him.

Funny how things worked out. Damned if it wasn't. A man schemed and dreamed and tried to pick up the cards as they fell and fit them to his hand, and then turned up an ace when he least expected it. Like this business of that twenty-four-year-old holdup coming to life again. Lay a loop on that phantom holdup man and he had a solution to his biggest problem. Just like that. But Purdy was the man with the answer, and Purdy had got away. Still, it was mighty interesting about the girl helping old Packrat get away; and when you got studying on that, it played into your hand, too.

Out by the cookshack, the supper bell rang, its sound clear and mellow. Torgin was reminded that he was hungry, but he was in no mood for the company of his crew. He got up and groped toward the kitchen, taking the bottle with him. Here he made himself a cold meat sandwich, washing it down with coffee which he laced from the whisky bottle. A heap of dishes strewed the drain. Maybe he'd better hire him another squaw one of these days. But that last one had gone babbling to Mannington just because he'd put a friendly hand on her, and a lot of people had treated him mighty cold for a time. Old Ma Hibbard had given him quite a piece of her tongue and threatened to lay a broom across his back. Well, the hell with all of them!

Better be thinking about that next move.

He stepped to the back door and opened it. Dusk lay thick in the yard, and the familiar buildings were vague silhouettes in the half-gloom. Some broken-down rolling stock littered the yard, busted wagons and scattered tire irons; and he reckoned he'd have to clean up out here, too, one of these days. He'd keep it in mind. A good part of the crew of ten who rode for him were seated on a bench before the cook shack, their after-supper cigarettes so many pin points of red. He raised his voice and shouted, "Hey, Gal!"

"Yes, Mack."

"Come on up to the house. I want to talk to you."

"Coming."

Torgin closed the door and found his way back to the parlor. He let himself down into the rocker again and waited. Growing impatient, he crossed the room to a corner table where stood a Graphophone, its morning-glory horn badly dented. From a litter of cylindrical records heaped beneath the table, Torgin chose one at random, gave the crank a few twists, and set the needle in the first groove. Minstrel music came to him, scratchy and raucous. This irritated him, and he stopped the machine and went back to his chair.

Gal was taking his own sweet time

coming. A funny one, that Gal. Sometimes, like now, Torgin got the feeling that having him around was like having a catamount by the tail. He'd been a lean and hungry one, Gal, that first night he'd come to the ranch, a porcupine prison haircut showing, and he'd made no bones about being busted out of Deer Lodge. He'd looked like he'd ridden the rods and slept in the haystacks, but he'd been good and brassy for all that.

"Friend of mine in stony lonesome hailed from hereabouts," Gal had said. "He told me Mack Torgin wouldn't be fussy about who he hired. You'll get a good thirty-a-month's worth out of me. I'll take my real pay in being covered up for a while."

That was how their acquaintance had started, Torgin remembered. Some of the crew hadn't liked his making Gal foreman when Gal hadn't been around even a month and a few of the old-timers had drawn Slash 7 pay for twenty-odd years. But Gal had a special skill — one that hung at his right hip. If a rancher were to broaden out, he could use that skill of Gal's and count the price as cheap. Yet the feeling always rattled around inside him that he owned only a small part of Gal.

Now he heard the front door creak to Gal's coming; and Gal entered, soft-stepping.

Torgin motioned with his hand. "Lay a fire and touch a match to it."

"I'm warm enough," Gal said and took a high stand near the fireplace. "What's on your chest?"

Torgin frowned and was of a mind to repeat his order, but he didn't. You got loyalty from Gal and the kind of thinking he could provide, and you couldn't go kicking that out the window just because Gal showed himself haughty sometimes. But it made you think again about that business of having a catamount by the tail.

Torgin said, "I've been sizing up the situation. Packrat Purdy's the answer to everything, but Purdy's gone skally-hooting. Still, Laura can't keep him hid forever. All we've got to do is lay low until a second chance shapes up. If I get Purdy in this house, I'll get the answer I want. He knows who stopped that stagecoach, and I'll bet Laura's guessed, too. That's why she helped him get out of the poky today."

Gal's face was lost in shadow, but his voice came clear and soft. "We could go looking up north tomorrow."

Torgin shook his head. "Too much country. I've got a better notion. I'll take a couple of the boys and go into Mannington tomorrow. I'd like a talk with Doc Brownlee. Maybe I've got enough aces in my fist to run a bluff on him. And maybe Laura will show back there. If she's going to keep Purdy hid, she'll want more to eat than cottontails. One way or the other, I may pick up something in Mannington."

Gal nodded and was suddenly a remote and thoughtful man, carried far from this room by his own dark brooding. "Mannington!" he said, an edge to his voice. "They had to name a whole damn town after him."

"Who?" Torgin asked absently.

"Manning."

Torgin came up out of the chair fast. "Gal, that's it!" he ejaculated.

"That's what?"

"Manning! Flint Manning. I've placed that stranger! He's old Flint's kid. Sure he is! Same face — same build — same voice. And he's just about the right age now. No wonder I was fooled. I was trying to place him for himself when all the time I was half remembering Flint."

Gal asked tonelessly, "Are you sure? Real sure?"

"Of course. When you mentioned the town, it came to me just like that."

Gal seemed to grow, to become a high and terrible shape there by the fireplace. He said in a rising voice, "And I had him in front of my gun, but you had to be standing in the way! You blundering damn fool! I had my chance and took your word that it wasn't the time or place. And now he's got away!"

Torgin said, "I don't understand," and was suddenly afraid, afraid of this anger of Gal's that filled the room, afraid of a wildness in the man that had somehow been touched off.

But Gal was leaving, heading hard for the door. Torgin ran after him, calling. Gal had left the door open. Torgin stood there, his eyes questing the darkened yard. He thought he made out movement in the horse corral. He called again and got no answer. In a matter of minutes hoofbeats pounded in the yard, and Torgin had then a brief

70

glimpse of Gal bent low over a saddle horn and heading for the trail that climbed out of the canyon.

Chapter Five

THE INVISIBLE WALL

Two things made Mannington different from other false-fronted log-and-frame towns of the mountain cattle country. One was the statue of Flint Manning that anchored the end of the main street and stood forever against the backdrop of the hills walling this south end of Bootjack Basin; the other was the brick charity hospital of Dr. Luke Brownlee, an institution whose fame had spread the width of Montana these past twenty years. But Cole Manning, wrapped in somber thoughts as he rode in at midafternoon, passed the monument to a man dead and the monument to a man living without giving either a great deal of attention.

He had awakened with last night's disappointment still brassy in his mouth, and he'd turned north again in spite of himself and spent a few hours scouting the vicinity where last he'd seen the girl. This empty searching had made his day no brighter, and now he looked with jaundiced eye upon the town that bore his name. The bronze likeness of his father was a mite idealized, he decided. And the hospital had got shabby with the years, the brick looking weathered and colorless and dusty. He could remember when they'd turned the first spadeful of dirt for the building, and there'd been speech-making and a band blaring and a lot of people milling under a hot sun.

He supposed the sight of Mannington should bring back a host of such memories and he should be moved by them. Somewhere along this street was the house in which he'd been born and lived the first eight years of his life, and he was surprised at how unerringly he picked it out. The place was now a millinery shop. Still, time had very nearly stood still in Mannington, he judged. The same dogs seemed to sleep in the street, the same creek racketed eternally beside the town; the same treetops brushed the same roofs. But he was a man now, bent upon man's business, and his first concern was to seek out Sheriff Burke Griffin. The jail building, which also housed the sheriff's office, was far along the street, near the outskirts. The structure was made of weathered logs and had a sagging porch before it, and on this porch sat the fattest man Manning had ever seen.

He filled a chair, that one. He was wedged down into it, and Manning got the impression that if the fellow jumped up suddenly, the chair would come with him. He had a round, apple-cheeked face and looked as though he should be behind the counter of a mercantile. He held a paper fan in one pudgy hand, and with this he idly kept the flies away.

He gave Manning a friendly grin and started to lift his free hand in greeting but let it drop as though the effort were too great. "Howdy," he said in a lazy voice.

Manning leaned forward, folding his arms upon the saddle horn. "Sheriff around?"

"I'm Griffin." The fat man sighed. "Forgot to pin on my badge this morning. The missus will likely fetch it when she comes to tell me supper's ready."

Faint irritation touched Manning. He'd found a hard bed in the basin last night, and for campfire company he'd had the remembrance of a day of frustrations. Then there'd been that futile search today. Now that he thought about it, the sight of his father's statue hadn't helped any, reminding him how Cole Manning was supposed to measure up. He said, "Do you think you could make it inside where we could do some talking?"

"I could try," Griffin said affably and got himself out of the chair with a mighty grunt. He waddled into the building; and Manning got down, wrapped the reins around a hitchrail, and followed him. The office was narrow and dusty and held a desk that looked like it had been knocked together from sluice-box lumber, a chair or two, and a dented Franklin stove. Time-yellowed, fly-specked reward dodgers, a frayed multitude of them, overlapped each other on the walls. Memories again rose and smote Manning, for he'd known this office well. Many times his father had led him here and perched him on this desk.

Griffin at once dropped into another chair, a counterpart of the one on the porch. He sighed. "Now what's your particular trouble?"

"I'm Cole Manning, Sheriff. I came to see Packrat Purdy. But it seems he's already pried the lid off this calaboose."

Griffin's only sign of surprise was the hoisting of a pair of mouse-colored eyebrows. Without rising, he extended a pudgy palm. "Young Manning, eh?" he said. "Been expecting you. Say, you favor your father a heap. You do, for a fact. I was deputy under him years back. Probably you don't remember me. I was a mite thinner then. Best buck and wing dancer in the Bootjack. You've growed a bit since those days yourself. Sit down, boy. Sit down."

Manning shook hands but remained standing. "I'd like to know how Purdy escaped."

Griffin sighed. "Plumb careless on my part." He looked up at Manning and grinned. "You recollect old Ma Hibbard, the cripple? No, I reckon you wouldn't. She cooks over at Doc Brownlee's hospital, and she's been fetching pies to Packrat. One a day, faithful as the clock. Me, I gave her a key and let her tote her pie back to the cell and chin with Packrat while he et. Well, sir, after she came hobbling out through the office yesterday, I had a look in Packrat's cell. And bust my britches if there wasn't Ma herself, sitting there in her petticoats. She'd give her dress and shawl and crutches to Packrat and let him walk out right under my nose!"

"Why did she do a thing like that?"

Griffin shrugged. "Couldn't guess."

"I'll have a talk with her," Manning said. "You've got her locked up?"

"Shucks, no. I gave her a scolding and sent her back to the hospital. Folks would be plumb peeved was I to keep Ma Hibbard jailed. Nearly everybody in town has been a patient at Doc's hospital at one time or another, and Ma makes a right tasty pie." He began to chuckle, his vast belly stirring. "The hurrawing that woman took for having to cross the street in her petticoats! A prim old gal, Ma. You'd have to know her to appreciate the humor of the situation."

Horsemen made a clatter out in the street. From where he stood, Manning could glance through the open doorway; and he recognized Mack Torgin, blocky in his saddle. Two men rode with him. Possibly they were two of the three who'd been involved in that pursuit yesterday, but neither of them was the man who'd interested Manning, the one called Gal. *They'll be over here in a minute,* he thought. *They'll come to tell*

Griffin how Purdy slipped through their fingers because of me. But they rode on. Manning stepped to the doorway and watched them. They swung along the street until they were in the region of the hospital, but when they got down from saddles, they headed toward the mercantile. Torgin, he noticed, seemed to be limping slightly.

He faced about and was again irritated by the bland face of Burke Griffin. "The jewelry that was found in Purdy's shack?" he asked. "You've still got it?"

Griffin indicated a locked desk drawer. "Sent an inventory to the Wells Fargo people. They wrote back and said it fitted the description on their old waybill. No doubt of it. I told 'em they could have it later, but we'd need it for evidence if you dabbed a loop on the jigger that stole it years back."

"How about the currency? A good many thousands of dollars were stolen at the same time, Griffin. No sign of *that*, or the mail, in Purdy's shack, eh?"

Griffin wagged his head. "Whoever robbed the stage knew he could spend the dinero, but he was likely scared the jewelry would be recognized. I'd guess that he hid the sparkly stuff, and Packrat found it and toted it home. Packrat ain't just right, you savvy. He's not crazy-loco, but his mind works like a ten-year-old's. You can bet he never had that money or he'd have gone on a spending spree years back, and Flint Manning would have nabbed him."

The street was comparatively quiet again, so quiet that Manning could clearly hear the brawling stream somewhere yonder. Whatever business had brought Mack Torgin to town, the man seemed in no hurry to get to the sheriff's office.

"Did you get any information out of Purdy?" Manning asked.

"Nary a bit." Griffin sighed again. "Packrat was some puzzled over being kept in jail. He's done a bit of stealing, but there's no real bad in him. We've always called it quits whenever we took things away from him and gave 'em back to the owners. It's been going on that way for nearly thirty years now. You're likely wondering why I ain't out chasing Packrat. I figger he'll show back by and by."

Some deep-stirred sense of the ridiculous came to Manning's rescue, making him less irritated. "You've been a great help, Sheriff," he said, but he didn't put any real bite into it. "Now I'll have to go and find out why Ma Hibbard pried Purdy out of the hoosegow."

"She'll talk a lot," Griffin prophesied. "She'll talk all day, for a fact. But when you sit down afterward and sort it out, I'll bet you'll find you ain't one minute brighter. Say, while you're over there, ask Doc Brownlee to send me some more rheumatism medicine when he gets time. I'll be mighty obliged."

"Sure," Manning said, straight-faced. "I'll even take a day off just to rub that medicine into you." He started for the doorway.

"Just a minute," Griffin called. "Almost forgot. There's a letter here." He pawed at the littered top of his desk and found an official-looking envelope. "Put this in your pocket and read it sometime when you're roundsiding. Came from the warden at Deer Lodge right after the papers started printing all that stuff about your taking the case that threw old Flint. You ever hear your dad mention a feller called Texas Joe Bridger?"

"Not that I recollect."

"Well, he was a killer Flint nabbed up

in the Marias country, after he'd un-pinned his badge and left here. Bridger drew a life sentence, but he busted out of stony lonesome not long ago. The warden got remembering that Bridger always held it against Flint Manning for putting him away. Maybe Bridger's es-caping at just this time means some-thing; maybe it don't. The warden reckoned you ought to be warned, though."

Manning stowed the letter inside his shirt. "Thanks," he said.

"You need any help," Griffin said, "you just come trotting to me."

"Oh, hell," Manning said and went out to his horse.

The sun stood low, and the town was beginning to mellow with twilight; and as Manning led his horse down the street, he was reminded that he was hungry. Leaving the horse at the first livery he found, he went in search of a restaurant. Those three Slash 7 horses were still tied near the hospital, he noticed, but Torgin was nowhere to be seen. Torgin's continued presence in town nagged at Manning, worrying him.

He turned into the first eating-place he came to and got a table to the back

81

and ordered. They put out a good steak in these parts, cut from beef made fat on mountain grass, but he had no real taste for it. Not this evening. He'd seen a last hope go winging, thanks to the stupidity of Sheriff Burke Griffin, who had neither managed to hold Purdy nor to wring any information from him. Or was the sheriff so stupid? Recalling his talk with Griffin, Manning got a notion that there'd been more than a lazy voice to Griffin. A lot more.

His meal finished, he came out to the boardwalk, tossed aside his toothpick, and let his gaze run the length of the street. At one edge of his vision, the bronze Flint Manning looked serenely and eternally on the town that was named for him. Only a few people showed at this supper hour — a couple of belated, bonneted shoppers, hurrying homeward, a half-dozen men idling beneath the wooden awnings. No one paid him heed. He smiled wryly, recollecting that he'd expected to be greeted by a brass band.

It was the loitering men who interested him, and suddenly he was struck by the enormity of his task. Any man past forty might have been that phantom holdup man of long ago. You could brush elbows with the fellow, never knowing. Even Burke Griffin could have been that ghostly one. You only had to hurdle yon western hills to Henry Plummer's country and take a peek back into Montana's history to be reminded that one man who'd represented the law had proved to be the worst of the lawless. Moreover, in talking to Burke Griffin, Manning had got the feeling that an invisible wall had been reared to keep him from the truth. What good then was there in going over to talk to Ma Hibbard, who in all likelihood would be just as evasive as Griffin?

But even as he pondered, he saw Mack Torgin walk alone from one of the saloons and go boldly toward the hospital and let himself in. At once Manning's interest was aroused. Torgin looked neither sick nor of the kind to dance attendance on the sick, and on impulse Manning crossed over to the brick building and eased inside.

He found himself in a shadowy corridor rank with the smell of medicine; and he moved quietly, conscious that this was a place of suffering, and conscious, too, that Torgin was somewhere about. In a distant room a woman groaned steadily, the sound a rasp against his nerves, and from another room came the wailing of an infant. He got his eyes accustomed to the gloom and stood hesitantly. To his left he found a door ajar; and when he peered, he saw that the door bore the legend: *Luke Brownlee, M.D. — Walk In.*

He had found the memories of his childhood spotty, had Manning. He'd not remembered Burke Griffin, but some things had stood out in bold clarity — the interior of the jail building, that celebration the day this hospital had been started, the house where once he'd lived — and he could also call up a clear picture of Luke Brownlee. Through the doorway he now had a glimpse of Brownlee at his desk, an older, grayer man than he'd remembered, but Brownlee for all that, with his glasses down at the end of his nose just as they'd always been. Manning might have stepped into the office, but the heavy voice of Mack Torgin stopped him.

". . . And if I do?" Torgin was saying. "I've got my plans too well along, Doc, to change them now. Look, you could

84

close your eyes to a few things, if you wanted. You're just out for my scalp!"

"Mack, you're wrong," Brownlee said wearily. "I'm going to put it plain to you. I've known you ever since you first came to the Bootjack. I've never cottoned to you, I'll admit, but there's nothing personal about this affair. Folks have made me county health official, and I've a job to do. You know that. And you've been buying low-priced cattle, and some of them have turned out to have tuberculosis. In spite of that, you've butchered some and sold the meat right here in Mannington. That's bad enough, but when you plan on putting in a packing-plant and making a fat profit by spreading death and disease, I've got to stop you. And I will. Either you drop your scheme, or I'll tell the whole basin what kind of cattle I've found on your range!"

"Hell, Doc, any rancher's bound to have a sick cow once in a while. You know that as well as I do. You're making a mountain out of this."

"Mack, you're wasting my time and yours."

A silence, long and ominous. Then: "Doc, here's something for you to think about. After the word came that Packrat

85

had escaped yesterday, I thought I saw Ma Hibbard hobbling out toward the edge of town. But when I got a good look, I knew confounded well it wasn't Ma. A wagon picked up that person. I got a few of my boys from the ranch and took out along the wagon road. I reckon maybe you know who was driving that wagon, Doc."

Brownlee drew the fingers of his right hand across his forehead. "All my life men like you have disputed the passage with me, Mack. If you're trying intimidation, it won't work. Go tell the law about your blasted suspicions!"

"And have Griffin blink at me and go back to sleep, eh? The whole damn town will side you, Doc, and you know it. But one of these days I may have something to hand them that even Griffin will have to heed. Just think that over, Doc!"

"Get out, Mack," Brownlee said wearily. "Get out of here, I say!"

Torgin took a step toward the door, and Manning heard him fumble for the knob. Silent as the shadows, Manning faded down the hallway, deeper into the building, until he came to the far end of the corridor and stood just outside an open doorway from whence came the clatter of dishes. He glanced behind him and saw Torgin shouldering out through the front door. He thought of the talk that had passed between Torgin and Brownlee and wondered what value he could find in it for himself. Something to think about, anyway. He looked through the doorway before him.

This was the hospital's kitchen; and from where he stood, Manning could see a lamp burning beyond and a plump, silver-haired woman seated in a chair by a table, busily wiping and stacking dishes. This was Ma Hibbard, no doubt of it. He stood there studying her, and that sense of futility he'd known on the street smote him again. He could step into the kitchen and have a talk with her, but he was remembering that invisible wall. You couldn't scale that wall, so you had to find a way around it.

So thinking, he stood there indecisively, and he saw Ma Hibbard come alert to some sound. At once his own curiosity was aroused. Another door, a back door leading into the kitchen from the alley, was creaking.

"*Laura!*" Ma Hibbard cried.

But she was no more astonished than Manning. Damned if the person who came stealing into the kitchen wasn't that Levi's-clad girl who'd driven the wagon for Purdy and later held forth on a cutbank with a six-shooter.

She stood there bold as brass with a finger raised to her lips. "Hush, Ma!" she was saying. "I came back to get more grub. Mack Torgin saw us leave Mannington and gave us a run. The grub sack must have bounced out of the wagon. Packrat was mighty worked up about that. For a little fellow, he's the eatingest man you ever saw."

Manning heard it all. Three quick strides, and he might have had his fingers wrapped around her wrist. Instead, he very quietly eased back up the corridor, a heady sense of triumph in him.

Dr. Brownlee's office door was still ajar as he passed it, and Brownlee still sat at his desk, apparently deep in thought, his shoulders hunched, a vague figure in the gloom. Coming out of the hospital, Manning cast a quick look along the boardwalk. No sign of Torgin. Running toward the livery stable, he got his horse, doing his own saddling in a frenzy of impatience; and soon he led the mount around to the rear of the hospital. Lamplight now sprang from many windows, and the shouldering hills were shapeless in the dusk. In the alley's depth, he waited in the deeper shadows, waited and watched.

His vigil wasn't long, but it was just long enough to bring the sweat to his palms and put a fear into him that his quarry had escaped while he'd been fetching the horse. Then, when he was fighting a temptation to enter the hospital for another look, the girl Laura came from the building, toting two heavy sacks roped together. The darkness swallowed her; a horse stomped and began to move away. Instantly Manning was jogging his own mount. For a moment he thought he'd lost the girl, but she angled around the corner of a building to the street and was revealed in a splash of light, a trim figure riding bareback on one of the horses that had pulled the wagon yesterday.

Over yonder, in the shadow of a porch, a man drew hard on a cigarette, and his face was thus briefly painted against the gloom. It was a long, saturnine face and a strange one to Manning. The cigarette went arcing, a tiny comet that hit the ground to lie unwinking like some malignant eye. The man laughed low in the shadows, and his boots went thudding against the boardwalk as he strode away, the sound remaining like a faint drumbeat after the night swallowed him.

But Manning paid no real heed to all this. His job was to keep his eyes on Laura up ahead, for Laura was going to lead him to Packrat Purdy.

Chapter Six

HUNTER HUNTED

Out of Mannington, the wagon road wound northward across far-reaching openness, with sometimes a fence breaking the shadow-swathed expanse. Here Laura moved at an unhurried pace; and here Cole Manning, after booming across the wooden bridge that spanned the creek at the town's outskirts, took up her trail. He kept at a discreet distance behind the girl, not wanting to alarm her. At first he rode slouched in his saddle, wanting to have the carefree look of a cowhand returning from town. That was in case Laura looked back. Soon he began worrying, for the road forked here and there, with offshoots running to the various ranches; and he was afraid she might take a turn without his knowing.

Cattle grazed at this end of the basin, sometimes cropping grass along the roadside, and Manning couldn't always be sure that what he sighted ahead was a horse. Yet reason told him that Laura would forge on northward, almost to the basin's far end, back to that country where he'd sought her yesterday and again this morning. But twice in the next hour he was certain he'd lost her. Each time he fought down a panicky impulse to gallop hard. Each time he sat his saddle for a long while, leaning forward and keening the night and sorting out its small sounds. Faintly there came to him the ring of shod hoofs against rocky outcroppings. So each time he moved on with a sense of relief.

The moon rose over the eastern rim of the basin, great and ghostly; and he could see the girl then, a remote figure up ahead. The land was becoming more broken, with intermittent tree clumps showing; and frequently his quarry vanished as she threaded sparse timber, all silver and shadow as the moon climbed higher. But the girl was staying with the old wagon road. Assured of that, Manning set a steady pace that kept him at the same distance behind her. Flint Manning, he told himself, couldn't have done a better job.

Within another hour he felt he must be near the spot where he'd first come off the slope to try to intercept the wagon the day before. He couldn't be sure, though. The land lay different at night, all illusion, its contours distorted. He passed through a clump of cottonwoods and was certain that here he'd unseated Torgin's bunch, but later he came to another cluster of trees that seemed exactly like the first. He could have looked for the rub of the rope, but he didn't waste the time. Still, he was irked at being so confused. The moonlit miles unreeled, bringing him into the tangled country of the north basin; and now he gradually closed the distance between himself and the girl, fearful that she might again elude him.

And that was when he became aware that someone was on the back trail.

At first he had only a whispered warning made more of instinct than reality. Once again he paused, his ears cocked, and he caught the faint ring of hoof against rock. Laura, up ahead? He tried hard to orient the sound and grew convinced that it rose behind him. Someone taking his trail or Laura's? Or some lone cowhand returning to a basin ranch? But there were no ranches this far north. He guessed he was developing an edge to his nerves, but he was mindful that Torgin had been in town.

93

Then, too, there was that stranger whose face had been so briefly revealed in the light of his cigarette. Come to look back on it, that one had had an air of watchful waiting.

He became a still man in the moonlight, his skin prickling to danger and a worry growing in him, for now he faced a new problem. Turn back and investigate the one who trailed him and thus risk losing Laura? He shook his head, not liking that notion. He moved onward, but in the next miles he was as attentive to the back trail as to the quarry ahead.

When next he glimpsed Laura, she'd come down off her horse and was leading the animal, picking a careful way westward through a maze of rocks and trees. Then, suddenly, she vanished. He moved closer, anger growing in him, and fear, and saw that she had entered a coulee so screened by brush that he might easily have passed its mouth. Tethering his own mount to a low bush, he crept after the girl.

Once again he had the feeling that he'd lost her, for the coulee seemed a brushy tangle with no sense to it. Wild roses grew here, and chokecherry bushes, concealing, for all he knew, a dozen coulees giving off this one. Then triumph rose in him, for he came upon the wagon; and when he peered hard, he made out openness ahead and saw the silhouette of the second horse, which seemed to be hobbled.

Bellying down to the ground, he lay watching. Laura was out there, too, hobbling the horse she'd ridden. He recognized her as she arose from this task. Slinging the grub bags over her shoulder, she continued on along the coulee; he heard bushes stir to her passage. He lay silent, letting the minutes tick by, his breath coming hard. He wanted to give her time to get well ahead before he came threshing after her. But not too much time! And while he waited, he wondered if the one who trailed them both had been thrown off the scent. No alien sound came to him from along the back trail.

Then he was up and moving forward. Now the moon was almost directly overhead, giving light enough to guide him, light enough to make him careful — mighty careful. The coulee began broadening out, and suddenly a dugout showed ahead, a crude structure of log walls built around a hole dug back into the coulee. No light showed from the dugout's one window. A good fifty yards of openness lay between Manning and the sagging door of the structure, but in the moonlight he saw Laura approach the dugout and heard the ancient hinges squeal as she opened the door. To the right of the dugout stood a corral, its poles fallen, its usefulness ruined. To the left was a big shed that had passed for a barn, and upon its side in painted letters large enough to be read at this distance was the legend:

Uncle Sam bet me I couldn't stick it out three years. Uncle Sam won!

Here, then, was a deserted homestead, abandoned by some pilgrim who'd brought a plow to the Bootjack and pitted it against rocky, forested land. You could find such monuments to foolhardiness all over Montana. But where one man had left his hope behind him, Cole Manning had found his; and a fierce jubilation rose in him. He'd tracked Laura to the hide-out where Packrat Purdy was being kept.

She was inside now, and it was safe

to cross to the door. He took a step toward the dugout. Then a new excitement crawled in him, for he heard a faint threshing behind and knew that someone moved through the bushes. Torgin? No matter who, he was again faced with a choice; and he made his decision fast. Turning around, he began moving carefully along the back trail, testing each step before he set down his boot.

In him desire cried to go on into the dugout and put Packrat Purdy under his gun, and this desire remained a steady torment even as he traveled in the opposite direction. Trouble was, you had to guard your back. You took on this job of being a professional man hunter, and though you'd inherited Flint Manning's looks and maybe some of his instinct for such work, you had to come by the rest of it the hard way. Once into that dugout, you might have your hands full — the memory of Laura's scrappiness yesterday was still fresh — and you didn't want someone else moving up on you from behind.

Hunter he'd been tonight, and hunter he must remain.

So thinking, he worked his way back

along the coulee, pausing often to listen. Now the one who hunted him was drawing nearer and not being too careful as he moved. Twigs cracked beneath the fellow's boots, and bushes swished to his passing. In the bright moonlight, Manning kept to cover and peered across an open space, wondering how to negotiate it; and as he looked, his man showed plain before him.

It was the one who'd watched and waited in Mannington and thrown his cigarette away when the waiting was ended. The one who'd gone striding away. No mistaking that long, saturnine face, even if you'd had only one glimpse of it. Now the man stood fully exposed, showing a long body to match that long face. Corduroy riding-breeches tucked into boots — a corduroy jacket to match the breeches — a string tie like a gambler's — a bit of white shirt showing — an expensive sombrero too wide of brim for this northern range. That was how the fellow added up.

His gun in his hand, Manning stepped out into the clearing and said sharply, "Just raise those paws, please," and saw quick surprise on the fellow's face.

But only for an instant. The man's hands went up, but his aplomb seemed scarcely shaken. He said, "You can put that gun away, Manning. It might go off, you know."

"And just who the hell are you?"

"The name is Ruxton — Slade Ruxton."

He had a voice in keeping with that sardonic face, a voice holding its hint of laughter. A cool one, this Ruxton. Manning stared at him, wondering if he'd heard the name before and growing sure that he hadn't. Two thoughts struck him. Ruxton looked to be somewhere in his thirties, which made him too young to have been that phantom holdup man of twenty-four years ago. The second thought was a mere hunch, but it grew to almost a certainty, and there was a way to put it to the test.

"Step back!" Manning ordered and waggled the gun. "Step back, I tell you!" When Ruxton obeyed, Manning moved forward, dropping to one knee and risking a glance over his shoulder to be sure they were out of sight and hearing of the dugout. With his left hand he fished out a match and thumbed it to life and held it close where Ruxton had just stood. The boot prints showed plain, and the sole of the left one was so worn as to leave a mark like a jagged star.

Manning stood up, fighting against anger. "So this makes our second meeting. What's your stake in this, mister?"

"The reward, naturally."

"What reward?"

Ruxton smiled. "It can't be that you really don't know. Wells Fargo posted a reward twenty-four years ago, right after that holdup. It still stands. Twenty-five thousand dollars for the arrest and conviction of that stagecoach robber or for proof of his death. It's a comfortable sounding sum, isn't it? That's why I'm in the Bootjack, and that's why I followed Laura Brownlee tonight."

"Brownlee!"

"Look, friend," Ruxton said, "are you pretending you didn't know she's old Doc Brownlee's granddaughter?"

Manning's thoughts were a chaos, but out of them came the remembrance of that heated talk between Torgin and Doc Brownlee at the hospital and Torgin's studied, intimidating, "I reckon maybe you know who was driving that wagon, Doc." So it had been Brownlee's granddaughter, along with old Ma Hibbard, who'd helped Packrat Purdy escape. Torgin had known that all along; and Torgin, selling diseased beef and fearing the pressure Doc Brownlee might bring to bear against him, had wanted a club to use against Brownlee. That was the size of it.

Or was it? Was Torgin hoping to capture Purdy that he might also capture Laura and prove her to be Purdy's accomplice? Or was something deeper involved, something that was an echo out of the yesterdays? Manning got the feeling that maybe the trail had turned more tangled, and all this while Ruxton stood smiling at him.

"How did *you* know her name, Ruxton? And mine, for that matter?"

"By most obvious means. In her case, I asked questions. Describe her to anybody in the basin and they'll hand you her name. As for you, I read the papers. And I've seen that statue in town. The papers said Flint Manning's son was en route; the statue gave me an idea what you'd look like. Two and two make four. As a badge toter, you're a little slow, friend."

"I'm a working apprentice," Manning said grimly. "Learning as I go."

"Then I think I could give you some lessons, Manning. I only got here half a day ahead of you, but it seems I've learned faster. Much faster. The vacuous Mr. Purdy appeared to be the key to everything, but it was my cursed luck to find him freshly absent from the jail. I rode out looking for him yesterday afternoon, pushing on till I got to this end of the basin. People were stirring about."

"So you took a few pot shots at me from the slope," Manning put in angrily. "And you wrecked my play for me. I'd have had Purdy but for that."

Ruxton half lowered his hands and shrugged slightly. "When I saw you tussling with that girl, I didn't know who you were, but both your voice and hers carried very well in this mountain air. You seemed much concerned about Purdy. Another bounty hunter, I thought. So I discouraged you."

"Because you wanted the reward for yourself?"

"For what other reason? The lady got clear away as a result of my gallant action, but at least the competition was eliminated for the time being. Not until I got a close-up glimpse of you in town tonight did I realize that I'd been inter-fering with the law. For that, I apolo-gize."

"Yeah," Manning observed, "with a grin spread all over your face."

"Obviously we're wasting time," Rux-ton said. "I judge that you trailed Miss Brownlee to her secret lair or you wouldn't be standing here exchanging experiences with me. Don't you think you'd better case that silly gun so we can get on to the important business? If you're interested in striking a bar-gain, I'll lend a hand at the *coup de grâce.* For half the reward — which is better than none. Is it a bargain?"

Manning put his gun in its holster but stood ready and wary. "It isn't the re-ward I'm after."

Ruxton shook his head unbelievingly. "So the papers intimated. Very well; the glory for you, the gold for me. I wouldn't have believed such an altruistic fool was left in the world."

"Then you've got something to learn, too," Manning snapped.

"You'll change your mind when the reward is within reach," Ruxton said. "But that's tomorrow's problem. Lead the way, Mr. Manning."

Cole Manning looked at him in the moonlight, seeing Slade Ruxton as something new in his experience, seeing a smart man who was single-minded but somehow smelled of unscrupulousness. He frowned. He could order the fellow to clear the hell out of here, he supposed; he could even arrest Ruxton for having interfered with a federal marshal yesterday, though that might be a hard one to make stick, considering that he'd been tussling with a girl when Ruxton had bought in. The other choice was to let Ruxton come along to the showdown. The whole question in that case was whether he could trust the man.

Ruxton might have been a mind reader. "You'll find a letter in my wallet. It's from the San Francisco office of Wells Fargo in answer to my inquiry as to whether the old reward still stands. Have a look at it."

"I'll take your word," Manning said.

"Then stop and consider that two cats closing in on one rat hole make for greater efficiency than one cat. Shall we get going?"

"Why not?" Manning said and moved along the coulee with Ruxton trailing

104

him. For the first few minutes, Manning's back was tensed and he wondered what sort of fool he was to take this risk. But Ruxton seemed content to follow peaceably, quieting down when Manning cautioned him to silence. Thus they came together to the clearing. A light now stood in the window of the dugout, and Manning whispered, "There it is."

"How do you intend to handle things?"

The laughter in that voice was like a sharp stick to Manning. "Like this!" he said and drew his gun again and sped swiftly across the clearing.

Ruxton was right behind him as he grasped the door, pulled it open, and lunged inside. There was only the one room, musty from long emptiness, and it held a crude table with the food sacks Laura had fetched piled upon it, a rusty cooking stove, two rickety chairs, a sagging bunk — no more furnishings than that. A lantern burned on the table, and in its light Manning saw Laura rise from one of the chairs, her face gone blank with surprise.

"Where's Purdy?" Manning demanded.

She moved back and stood crouched

against the rear dirt wall; she shook her head numbly, the fear in her eyes telling Manning that she recognized him from yesterday.

"First you've got to know that I'm not one of Torgin's men," he said. "I'm Cole Manning, federal marshal. This man is Slade Ruxton, here because of Wells Fargo. You've got to tell us where Purdy is!"

"Gone," she said tonelessly, and swept her hand to take in the whole dugout. "He was gone when I got back tonight. Torgin's found him, I think."

"Are you telling the truth?"

"Of course she's telling the truth," Ruxton said at Manning's elbow. "Can't you see that she's almost in a state of shock?" He was the cool one again, turning a thoughtful face to the girl but not showing any pity. In this moment Manning found something to admire in him, for Ruxton was taking disaster in his stride. Ruxton's smile returned. "I shall leave you to comfort the lady, Mr. Manning. Good night, both of you. The deck seems to have been reshuffled. Good luck — and the full reward to the man first able to claim it."

He was gone, bobbing out through the

doorway so suddenly that the lantern flame made a throaty sound in its chimney with his passage.

Chapter Seven

WILD MAN RIDING

In Gal, riding wildly from Slash 7 the night before, one thought beat steadily as he spurred his horse. *Get Manning! Get Manning!* This was a relentless drumming in him, drowning out all other thought till he realized he was quirting the horse up the steep slant to the canyon's rim. He eased down then, though his turmoil was no less; and when he got higher and hipped around for a look at the buildings below, he found that his hands were shaking, and he was breathing as though he'd run a hard mile. He'd have to get hold of himself, he decided. He mustn't let the old craziness make his judgment unsteady, too.

Yet anger stayed. Damn Mack Torgin for a blind, stupid blunderer! Why hadn't Torgin recognized Cole Manning when he'd stood within reach out there in the cottonwoods? Manning, as a stranger, hadn't meant much, though Gal would have got in a lick with his hide-out gun if Torgin hadn't halted the play. But there would have been nothing personal about it. Not then. Turning all this over in his mind, it struck Gal that he should be glad that Torgin *had* interfered. If Manning had died that afternoon, he'd have died not knowing who'd cut him down. That wouldn't have pleased Gal. Not the way he'd take his pleasure when he again stood face to face with Cole Manning.

This thought stayed with him to the top of the rise and sent him galloping hard once he was on level ground. He cut for the wagon road and headed due north, riding recklessly and cursing the darkness that made the trees something you didn't see until you almost piled into them. There might be badger holes, too. He looked to the hazy, lifting outlines of the eastern hills and saw that a cloud rack obscured the sky. No chance of moonlight to help him. Not tonight. He blundered along until he came to a clump of cottonwoods that might well be the one where he'd been spilled. He climbed down and spent a match and saw enough sign to convince him that this was indeed the place.

Climbing back on his foam-flecked horse, he sat rigidly, feeling hog-tied.

Those Slash 7 boys who'd walked back here to pick up the guns had reported that Manning had vanished. Stood to reason that Manning had headed north, for Slash 7 had gone the other direction and Manning hadn't showed on their trail. Manning must have set out after Laura Brownlee and Packrat Purdy. That was it. The damn badge toter had sure got a good jolt when he'd learned who'd been in the wagon! Gal drew some satisfaction from that, and part of the haze lifted from his brain.

He'd given his horse a hard go. Suddenly he felt sorry for the horse and considered himself a mean one for having used the mount so.

He reached out and patted the horse and brought his hand away wet. Crazy, the way he'd ridden. What was it the prison doctor used to say to him in those early years at Deer Lodge when he'd got those wild spells and had to be put in solitary? "You're not really crazy, Bridger, any more than I or the warden or anybody else. Each of us has got some one sore spot that makes us come off the hinges when it's touched. Yours is your hate for Flint Manning. You get thinking about his putting you here, and your hate sprouts like a poisonous weed. But the only person it harms is you."

Well, he'd got that sore spot touched tonight when Mack Torgin had suddenly remembered who Cole Manning was. Maybe he shouldn't even hold that against Mack, considering that he, too, had had a look at young Manning and therefore a chance to remember. The kid favored his father enough; that was certain. But he, Gal, hadn't neighbored with Manning eight years here in the Bootjack as Torgin had. Still, as little as he'd seen of Flint Manning, Gal would have sworn that that high-boned face, big-beaked and smoky-eyed, was stuck in his memory forever. Sometimes, like now, it stood before him real clear.

The trouble was that after eighteen years a lot of faces began to run together — Manning's and the judge's at Shelby and the pinched face of that pip-squeak lawyer they'd assigned to defend him in the courtroom. Then, too, there was all the parade of faces across those years in stony lonesome — the old ones and the young, the lifers and those who'd stayed briefly and gone

111

beyond the gate. It wasn't the shape of a man's nose that stuck with you; it was what he'd done to you and what you had to do back to him and his.

A breeze ruffled the leaves of the cottonwoods, and he shivered in spite of himself. The wind's whispering was like the whispering of men in the cell blocks, lost and forlorn and not quite human.

Gal jogged his horse and began riding northward, not trying to cut sign, for he knew how useless that would be. He was just lazing along, hoping — hoping — He wished for moonlight and tried to remember what the almanac had said, last time he'd looked into it; but he guessed it didn't matter, considering that cloud rack. The air smelled of rain, but the rain held off. The hills bulked around him and the miles unreeled, and something of calmness came back to him. Maybe, just by chance, he'd stumble upon another rider of the night. He had been patient for a good long time; he could be patient still.

Shucks, he could even wait for daylight when the searching would be easier and Manning would more likely be abroad. He'd been veering a little eastward, toward Bootjack River. He headed now for the willows along that stream, pulled into them, squaw-hobbled his horse, and spread the saddle blanket upon the ground and used the saddle for a pillow. A little too early in the season for the mosquitoes to be pesky, and he liked the sound of running water so close by.

He got to thinking of Deer Lodge again as he waited for sleep to come, smoking a last cigarette and looking up through the interlaced branches at the sky. That's what he'd missed most in stony lonesome — the sky. That Deer Lodge valley was beautiful enough, framed by Mount Powell and a ring of pine-clad hills, but they seldom let you beyond the walls so you could get a real look. All you got was a chunk of sky overhead; and you began to wish that you'd served your time on an earlier day when the prisoners were sent under guard to the near-by mountains to quarry the stone from which the walls and towers were built. Hard labor, but at least it had allowed some elbow room. A Texan needed room. In the later day that he'd known, you worked on saddles or lolled around the prison library; but even though your fingers and eyes were busy, you could do your own thinking, and always you thought of Flint Manning — and escape.

And then Flint Manning had fooled you by dying.

In the darkness of the Bootjack, Gal crushed out his cigarette and thumbed it into the ground, feeling that wild, reckless anger rise again. He fought it down with an effort, not helping himself much by letting his mind hark back to that day in the prison library when he'd read the newspaper accounts of Flint Manning's passing. Column after column they'd had about Manning, full of fine phrases like . . . *died for his country and the glory of his flag,* even though Manning had turned up his toes in some pesthole of a camp in Georgia. They'd gone back to his trail-town days to dig up every bit of his record, and they'd splashed it on with a broad brush. There'd even been a paragraph about Gal at the very end. Gal had read it enough times so that he could have recited it now.

. . . Though Manning had retired as a law officer when he moved with his family to the Marias country in 1892 and took up the peaceful pursuits of a rancher, he

was once again called upon to assume the role of man hunter. An outbreak of rustling in the vicinity culminated in the murder of a stockman in 1894, and Manning was invited to join the posse. He elected to work alone and, single-handed, captured Joe Bridger, youthful rustler who had recently come from Texas. Bridger was convicted of murder and sentenced to life imprisonment in Deer Lodge, where he is still serving time . . .

Gal rolled over now and put an ear to the saddle. Four years he'd been in prison when he'd read that account, and he'd turned into a wild man again with the knowledge that Manning had slipped beyond him. But Manning's family still remained. That was the thought he'd clung to. There'd been a wife mentioned in those newspaper accounts, but something in a Texan's code forbade carrying his war against a woman. But there was also a son, aged fourteen, and that son would one day be a man, looking like his father, probably, and thinking like his father, and answerable for the thing his father had done.

That thought had grown in Gal across

the next decade, and always he'd dreamed of escape. Then there'd been an abortive prison break in '08, with a deputy warden killed and Conley, the warden, wounded; and two prisoners had been hanged in the prison yard for their little frolic. That had given Gal something to chew on. No sense ending up doing an air dance just because you itched to get over the wall. He'd learned how to hold onto himself, and only once in a great while had he got those wild spells such as had put him in solitary those first years until the prison doctor had told him about that kink in him.

It was the newspapers that came into the prison that really set Gal off again. There'd been that journalistic hullaba-loo about an old holdup case in the Bootjack country coming to life again, and there it was in black and white how Cole Manning was stepping into his father's boots to take a try at succeed-ing where Flint Manning had failed.

Gal had read it all. The holdup hadn't interested him. It had happened before he'd even come to Montana, and the satisfaction he'd got came from know-ing that Flint Manning had once failed. Not that he couldn't have told the papers a few things about the great Flint Manning that would have opened people's eyes, only the papers weren't printing the mouthings of convicts. Not by a damn sight! The interesting thing to Gal was that Cole Manning had now come into the case. Cole Manning — aged twenty-eight — was en route to the Bootjack, and that was where a man could find him.

So Texas Joe Bridger, alias Gal, had walked away from Deer Lodge penitentiary.

It had been as easy as that. These last years they had made him a trusty and sometimes allowed him the privilege of going into the town. His job that last day had been to take flowers to the prison section of Hillcrest cemetery, and his only fetter had been his pledged word to return. Funny how hard it could hit a man to have to break his word. He hadn't liked doing that, but there was the memory of one Manning and the thought of another, and he'd just kept walking. After that he'd hidden by day and traveled by night, and holed up in Butte for a while, and thus he'd come at last to the Bootjack and Mack Torgin's door.

And today he'd stood face to face with Cole Manning.

He carried that remembrance with him into sleep and was awakened by the sun filtering through the branches to touch his face. He was hungry, but he put his mind against hunger. He caught up his hobbled horse and saddled and hit the trail, moving westward and northward.

Now at least he could see where he was riding. He kept forging on, sidetracking to explore coulees, pausing often to lean forward in his stirrups and listen for any sound that might tell him of another horsebacker in the vicinity. Sometimes he came across sign — clear prints in the ground and the droppings of horses and the black scars where fires had been built, but always the sign looked too old.

By early afternoon he was feeling frustrated and weary and much hungrier than before, but still he persisted, riding aimlessly. The bigness of the Bootjack was a scary thing; he was too used to confining walls; and the bigness might keep him forever from Cole Manning. This thought haunted him.

He tried putting himself in Manning's

place and thinking as he supposed Manning would think; and he judged that if Manning's search were as futile as his own, he'd probably turned south to the town. Gal had made a great point of not showing himself in town, mindful that there was a cell waiting in Deer Lodge. He was tempted now, but he was not such a wild man as to be an unwary one. He could wait.

So thinking, he suddenly stiffened to alertness, for he heard someone riding near by.

He was in a stand of aspen part way up the west slope, and from here he could look down upon a stretch of fairly open country. The sound of that on-coming rider grew louder; and Gal, peering, reached and moved his holster to a ready position. Yonder was Manning, he was sure, and he was surprised at the rock-steadiness of himself. He knew exactly what he would do and exactly what he would say, and the words would be important, too. Quick, harsh words that built in him now — words that would let Cole Manning know what it was all about before the fireworks started. Words that had been eighteen years in the readying, for once they were to have been spoken to Flint Manning.

And then the horsebacker came into view, and disappointment was like a hard blow to Gal's stomach. For she was Laura Brownlee riding bareback on one of the horses that had pulled the wagon yesterday.

She was down there in full range of his vision, and she was heading southward, heading toward town. Going after grub, he supposed, for she had some empty gunny sacks tied together behind her.

Gal could go roaring out of the aspens and get her under his gun, if need be, and he was tempted. He remembered how Mack Torgin had come storming to the ranch yesterday, all excited and babbling about Packrat Purdy's heading into the basin in a wagon driven by Laura Brownlee. He knew about Torgin's packing-plant scheme and how Doc Brownlee stood in the way of it, and thus he also knew what an opportunity it had made for Torgin to find Laura Brownlee involved in a jail break. Full proof might have brought Doc Brownlee to his knees, but Cole Manning had come along and fouled up the chance.

Now Doc's granddaughter was within reach, and opportunity knocked again.

All this passed through Gal's mind, and all the decency in him dictated that he capture Laura Brownlee for Mack Torgin's sake. Damned if he didn't owe Torgin something. Yet his own need was greater — that frenzied need to line sights on Cole Manning. Go grabbing the girl and you lost your chance for further searching today. That was what the choice amounted to, and while he wrangled it in his mind, Laura rode on south and was soon out of sight.

He rode onward then, coming back to the basin's floor and continuing his endless prowling. Yet now he had a wrong taste in his mouth, something like he'd had when he'd got clear of Deer Lodge by breaking his word, only this was even bitterer.

Once he'd been a cowboy, long ago in Texas, and he'd got it ingrained that you stayed loyal to your boss. He thought of himself coming to Torgin's door of a night and laying his cards on the table for Torgin, admitting he was fresh out of stony lonesome and on the dodge. He thought of Torgin's giving him shelter and putting him on the payroll and thus making it possible for him to stay in the Bootjack till Cole Manning showed. He hadn't told Torgin about his driving need, not tipping his true hand a bit until last night, when he'd gone wild with the realization that Manning had been within reach. Now he could see that the whole business, his need and Torgin's, was tied together, really; and he'd been disloyal.

He was heading almost due north, following a ridge between two coulees. He could look down into the brushy sides of either ravine. He moved along slowly, holding the horse to a walk and picking a careful way, and when he made one of his periodical stops to listen, he heard movement in the brush of the coulee to his right. Again excitement stirred him, but he'd known disappointment once and was prepared for it a second time. *Maybe a deer*, he thought. He came down from the saddle and let the horse stand with trailing reins.

There it was again, a faint stirring. The right-hand coulee, for sure. He edged forward carefully and began climbing down into the coulee. A shallow creek bubbled in its bottom, and through the fringing willows he caught a glimpse of movement. He drew his gun as he stole closer, then put it away, knowing he wouldn't need it.

A man was down on his knees beside the creek, filling a battered, rusty bucket. Gal had had no more than a fleeting glimpse of Packrat Purdy yesterday, but he knew him now. Stripped of Ma Hibbard's dress, Purdy proved to be a short oldster with a shaggy mop of hair and a simple face. A useless-looking man, Purdy; it was funny, sort of, to think of his being valuable to anybody. He was so intent upon filling the bucket that he was unaware of Gal's presence till Gal said softly, "Howdy."

Purdy might be slow of wit, but he knew danger when he saw it. He stood up at once, a man half ready to run, half ready to fight, yet not really able to do either. And Gal, looking at him, knew now what he must do for Mack Torgin, having been given this second chance.

He said, "Come along, Packrat. We're going to Slash 7, you and me." And only by Purdy's alarmed face could he tell how deadly his voice must have sounded.

Chapter Eight

INTO THE CANYON

In the silence following Slade Ruxton's departure, Cole Manning stood in the lantern-lighted dugout with Laura Brownlee and felt the first shock of disappointment at finding Packrat Purdy gone. Any way you looked at it, another trail had dead-ended. Ruxton's quick acceptance of the fact and his hurrying away to pick up the scent again had dispelled Manning's last hope. Laura wasn't lying.

Manning glanced at her again, and seeing the defeat in her face, and the weariness, suddenly felt sorry for her. He told himself sternly that he mustn't be overwhelmed by such a feeling. She was, he remembered, the law breaker, and he was the man with the badge.

Now what the hell did you do in a case like this? You couldn't go clapping the handcuffs on a girl — especially when you didn't carry any handcuffs — and you couldn't go making tough talk just to show her who was boss. Couldn't even take her gun away from her, for no gun was in evidence; apparently she hadn't risked going back to the cutbank for the one he'd wrested from her yesterday.

His sense of the ridiculous rose, and he asked, making his voice gruff, "Why do you think it was Torgin who found the old fellow?" He was remembering that Torgin had been in Mannington most of the afternoon. Besides, Laura was the one Torgin was after, wasn't she, not Purdy.

She spread her hands in a tired gesture. "Packrat would be around here if he hadn't been nabbed. Last night he slept in the barn. I've looked out there. He's gone."

"Any place else he might have gone?"

She thought about that, her pretty face reflective. "For water, perhaps. The well here caved in, from the looks of it. There's a creek in the next coulee."

"Let's go and see," he said and lifted the lantern from the table. "Maybe he fell asleep under a tree."

She came with him. He should take hold of her wrist, he supposed, to make sure she didn't bolt, but she gave no sign of wanting to escape. To her the most important thing seemed to be

Packrat's absence; she was as eager as he to find the old eccentric. With the lantern swinging between them, and their shadows scissoring along, it was she who found the trail that hairpinned up the slope of this coulee and down into the other. He saw the palisading willows and heard the murmur of the creek and moved toward it. He lifted the lantern high and moved it in a wide arc. At the creek's bank, they found the battered old bucket.

"Recognize this?" he asked.

She nodded. "It was in the dugout." Her eyes were reflective; she hadn't showed fear since he'd named himself.

Bending low, he held the lantern close to the ground. In this manner he circled, peering, always peering. He was, he knew, no Flint Manning when it came to reading sign; and he supposed that he cut a silly sort of figure, doubled over like the rheumatism had got him, but he began to piece out a story from what he saw. His investigation took him up the trail to the ridge between the coulees, and then he came back to where Laura waited by the creek.

"I think I've got it," he said, "though the tracks run all over each other. A horseman came here, left his mount up on the hogback, and walked down to Packrat. The two of them climbed the ridge together afterward and rode off on the horse."

"Torgin," she said firmly.

He shook his head. "Torgin was in town."

"One of his men, then."

"Maybe."

They climbed back into the other coulee, but here Manning swung southward, saying, "Come along." They trudged the coulee to its far end, where Manning had left his tethered horse. He led the mount back and put it in the wrecked corral. He set down the lantern, not really needing it for anything but close-up work with the moon so bright, and lifted enough of the poles back into place so that the corral would hold. This did not take him long. Laura watched him silently. He said, "You could have done this and kept your team here."

"I thought of it," she said. "The team's better off where it is. That way, if someone came upon the wagon and horses, they still might not have found the dugout. But if they found the horses here, they'd wonder who was in the dugout."

"Smart enough," he conceded.

He went inside the dugout and put the lantern on the table; he sloshed the lantern absently to see how much coal oil remained. Enough. She must have fetched the lantern in the wagon yesterday, and likewise the blankets he saw on the bunk. A thorough girl, this Laura Brownlee, and a hard one to figure. With the light on her just so and her hair tumbled down, she looked like a wildling who'd dart away at the passing of a shadow; yet he'd found her ready with a gun and bolder than any hawk. Trouble was, you couldn't tell what was going on inside that pretty head. Not for sure.

"That man Ruxton?" she asked. "Is he your partner?"

Manning grimaced. "He was for a while tonight. He's after the bounty Wells Fargo put up for that holdup man. I don't think Slade Ruxton trusts anyone very far."

"And do you?"

He shrugged.

"I'm sorry I bit and scratched you yesterday." She made her blue eyes soften, but he guessed her contrition was genuine. "I thought you were Torgin's new man. We've heard that there is one, but he never shows in town."

"Fellow with a pair of blue eyes like ice?"

"I've never seen him, not close, anyway."

"You believe that I'm Cole Manning, don't you?"

"You look like the statue, now that I've had a chance to study you. And we've known you were coming. Yes, I believe you. Why don't you go back to the Marias where you belong?"

"Why don't you tell me why you framed it up with Ma Hibbard to bust Packrat out of jail? I'll bet the whole scheme was yours."

"You wouldn't understand."

"Try me!"

She shook her head. "You work hard at being a very grim young man. I think I know, just from having read the papers, why you're so determined to break that old case. You want to stand higher than Flint Manning. I didn't know him, of course, but I've heard Gramp talk about him. I don't think you've got enough rawhide to outdo your father. And that's why it sours you just to think about him."

This appraisal struck close enough to home to anger him. "And you're a very smart young lady who thinks she can go skylarking around breaking people out of jail. I don't know whether to turn you over my knee or haul you back to Mannington and lock you up."

She canted her head and smiled at him. "And what evidence have you against me, except your own word?"

He thought about that with growing exasperation until a bigger thought grew from the first, and he snapped his fingers. "I've got it!" he cried. "I saw a glimmer of the truth when Slade Ruxton told me you were Doc Brownlee's granddaughter. If Purdy got dragged off to Slash 7, Torgin will try to make him talk. It's evidence Torgin wants. If Purdy can be made to admit that *you* engineered his escape, then Torgin can put Doc Brownlee over a barrel. You see, I know that your granddad stands between Torgin and his packing-plant scheme."

"How do you know that?"

He grinned. "I eavesdropped. I put my ear to a keyhole while Torgin was trying to intimidate Doc."

She nodded. "You're right, as far as

you've gone. And now what are you going to do?"

His grin broadened. "*We* are going to get a good night's sleep," he said. "You in the bunk, and me here by the doorway to make sure you don't walk in your sleep. When we're fresh as a pair of mountain flowers, we'll go riding. Once I've got you safely locked up in the Mannington jail, I'll pay a little business call on Mack Torgin and show him my bright new badge. After we've discussed the weather and the crops, I'll ask him if he wishes to continue obstructing justice by holding Purdy prisoner. Then I'll point out that he can relieve himself of a burden by turning Packrat over to me. How does that sound?"

She shook her head; she looked very tired. "You'll keep hunting and hunting, I know. Till you come to the end of the trail. And then it will be too late for you to see that you should never have started."

"What kind of riddle is that?"

"Cole, go back to the Marias!"

"Better get to bed," he said.

He left the dugout and went to the decrepit old barn and found the blankets Packrat Purdy had used. He gathered these up. By the time he returned to the dugout, the lantern had been extinguished, and he heard the soft movements of Laura in the bunk. He was stirred by her nearness and thought this an odd thing, remembering that she was part of that invisible wall that barred him everywhere in the Bootjack. He spread the blankets by the doorway and shucked out of his boots and chaps and unlatched his gun belt. He climbed into the blankets and lay in the darkness and said at last, softly, "Laura?"

"Yes?"

"Why don't you tell me why it was so important to get Packrat out of jail? You wanted him gone before I showed up to talk to him. Isn't that it?"

She sighed. "Maybe it was because Flint Manning and Doc Brownlee were very good friends long ago."

"What's that got to do with it?"

A long silence. Then: "Good night, Cole."

He turned over in his blankets, knowing the uselessness of further talk. He sought sleep, but he found himself taut, all the people he'd encountered since coming to the Bootjack parading through his mind. He saw Torgin and Gal and Laura and Packrat Purdy; and when his mind wandered to this afternoon in town, he heard again the voices of Burke Griffin and Doc Brownlee and Ma Hibbard. He banished them one by one and half dozed; and in his mind's ear rang those ghostly hoofbeats out of the long ago, the faint, dying echo of that phantom holdup man's horse. The illusion was so vivid that it brought him fully awake, but the only real sound was the soft breathing of Laura and the murmur of a breeze in the treetops.

He tried dozing again and thought of Slade Ruxton, gone to follow his own fancy, gone with the belief that no man took a trail for other than the hard round dollars at the end of it. And thinking of Ruxton, he fell asleep.

He awoke with a feeling of strangeness, not at once remembering his whereabouts and seeing only the sagging roof overhead. He stared upward until he recognized the place. Then he hastily flung aside his blankets and lunged toward the bunk, expecting to find Laura gone.

She was dressed and seated on the

edge of the bunk, combing out her long tawny hair. She looked up at him, smiling faintly, and said, "I guess we both slept late. If you'll get a fire going, I'll make some breakfast."

"Sure," he said.

He was sour-minded and sore-bodied; for it had been hard bedding there on the floor, harder than he'd found it in the basin, where he'd had the grass between him and the ground. He could have cut some pine boughs to make a mattress last night, and now he wished he had, but he'd hesitated to wander too far from the dugout, leaving Laura alone.

Boots and belt donned, he rattled the stove lids and picked kindling from a box that had probably been kept filled by the elusive Purdy. He looked about for paper and remembered the letter inside his shirt, the one from the warden, the one Sheriff Burke Griffin had given him. He used the envelope to get the fire started; and while Laura rummaged in the food sacks, he sat down to give the letter a quick skimming:

. . . *Joseph Bridger, known as Texas Joe Bridger . . . born in Galveston, Texas . . . former cowboy . . . convicted of*

*murder and rustling at Shelby in 1894
. . . in early prison years evidenced a
great hatred for Flint Manning . . . escaped recently . . . six foot one and a half
. . . one hundred and eighty pounds . . .
light hair . . . blue eyes . . . model
prisoner in many respects . . .*

Manning folded the letter and thrust
it into his pocket, his eyes thoughtful.
1894. He'd been — let's see — ten years
old then.

Lately he'd learned just how tricky
memory could be. Here was another
sample. He could remember things
from the early Bootjack days, yet this
later event had escaped him completely.
But now that he thought about it, frag-
ments of recollection began piecing
themselves together. There was that
group of grim-faced riders who'd come
to the Marias ranch and talked to his
father in the yard. That must be the
time his father had been gone for so
many days and his mother had paced
the floor and peered from the windows
and stood in the yard evenings, looking
to the far horizons till it grew too dark
to see. His father had come home, but
whatever he'd had to say had been for
his wife's ears only. Thereafter he'd

gone again, a few weeks later, and Cole Manning remembered asking about that and being told that his father had gone to testify in court.

"How do you like your eggs?" Laura asked.

"Straight up," he answered absently.

Testify. So that had been the time when Flint Manning had tracked down Texas Joe Bridger and helped send the man to Deer Lodge for life. An unofficial job, according to Burke Griffin; and that made sense, too, for Flint Manning had shucked his badge two years before.

The smell of coffee rose in the dugout, and Manning saw Laura busying herself before the stove. He heard bacon sizzling, and a short time later she called him to the table. He ate absently, his mind still working at that letter, and then it hit him. Gal! There was a queer name for a man to be packing, though once or twice in his life Manning had heard of people with such a surname. But Gal could also be short for Galveston, the place of Texas Joe Bridger's birth. Six foot one and a half. A hundred and eighty pounds. Blue eyes. Yes, it all fitted.

"I think," he said slowly, "that I'll have two jobs to do at Slash 7."

She made a face. "So you're a lawman the last thing before you go to sleep and the first thing when you get up."

He judged that she was laughing at him, though only her eyes showed it. She was a calm girl today, and a friendlier one; and he was reminded that he had a day's beard and must look a sight. He said, grinning, "Do you sometimes go dancing or buggy-riding with the boys? Or do you spend all your time breaking old coots out of jail?"

She said, "If you ever get shed of the thing that drives you so hard, came around and ask me then."

He shoved back his plate and drained his coffee cup. "Time to get going," he announced. "It must be near noon." He walked over to his discarded chaps and climbed into them.

When he'd saddled and helped her up behind him, they rode down the coulee to where she'd left the team hobbled and the wagon standing. He frowned, facing a problem. He could hitch up the team and have Laura drive the wagon back to town, but they would have to stay with the wagon road, and he wasn't sure that would be wise. Suppose Torgin should be abroad with his bunch and come a-roaring at them before there was a chance to flash a badge in the man's face? He and Laura were already handicapped by riding double, but at least they wouldn't have to keep to the road.

He turned the various factors over in his mind and then suggested that she ride one of the team bareback as she'd done yesterday. She fashioned a hackamore from a bit of rope in the wagon, and shortly they were jogging along side by side.

"Rather sit a saddle?" he asked.

She shook her head. "I like riding Injun style."

He had only a general idea where Slash 7 lay, remembering vaguely that it was along the west wall and toward the south end of the basin, somewhere this side of Mannington. He asked Laura, and she described the canyon and the trail leading into it.

Thereafter they moved in silence through the somnolent afternoon, seeking out the dim, pine-scented trails; and they might have been alone in a vast world of rock and sky and timber.

They came across the miles in a communion of silence, with some intangible nagging at Manning from which he tried to shut his mind, some nameless feeling toward Laura that made the thought of her in Mannington's jail a dark one. He had been bred to the law, but he'd never pondered the limitations of the law. He caught Laura's profile from the corner of his eye and saw that she was troubled, too.

In late afternoon, when they'd dropped to the basin's floor again and were crossing openness, she pointed west. "See that clump of trees?" she said. "Head through them and you'll find yourself on the trail that drops down to Slash 7. You'll need to know so you can find your way when you come back from town."

He drew rein and was careful not to look at her. "I'm not going to take you on to town," he said gruffly. "We part here. I'm going to Torgin's."

He felt her eyes on him. "What changed your mind?" she asked.

"Hell," he said, "Burke Griffin would only scold you and turn you loose. Why should I waste the time?"

"Then I'm going with you to Slash 7."

"No!" he snapped, and that one word was wrung out of something akin to fear.

He turned and spurred his horse to a gallop, heading toward the trees she'd indicated. Into them, he found that she had pounded along hard behind him. He gave her an angry glance. He rode on through the trees and was nearly to the rim of the canyon when he drew rein again. He looked at Laura and said gently, "It's a man's work. You'd only be in the way."

She leaned forward, laying a hand on his arm, her face showing faint alarm. "Cole, you're pinning too much faith on a badge," she said intently. "Suppose Mack Torgin isn't of a mind to let Pack-rat go and decides to keep you prisoner, too. He's capable of it. Have you thought of that?"

"Yes," he said. "But I'll chance it."

"Name a time," she urged. "Tell me how long you think it will take to do your chore down there. I'll wait up here. If you're not back when you expect you'll be, I'll go for help."

She was very serious about this; and looking at her, he saw now what had been plain from the first if only

140

he'd had the eyes for it. She was no flibbertigibbet who ran the basin's wilds with Packrat Purdy for the fun of it. Whatever motivated her went deep and was made of some trait admirable and selfless that made his own actions seem petty. He remembered what she'd said about the friendship between Flint Manning and Doc Brownlee, and he wondered if her present concern for him was made from that. He hoped not. Whatever she had for him, he wanted it to be for himself alone. He had walked too long in the shadow of Flint Manning.

But she was awaiting his answer. "Very well," he said. "If I'm not back by sundown, you'll know it's because I can't come back. So long, Laura."

"So long, Cole," she said and lifted her hand and let it fall.

He jogged on past her and dipped into the canyon. When he looked back, he was below the rim and she was lost to sight; and the odd thing was that he was suddenly lonely.

Chapter Nine

THE MAN WHO SCHEMED

Earlier this day, while Cole Manning and Laura Brownlee had prepared to ride south toward Slash 7, Slade Ruxton had left the vicinity of Torgin's ranch and turned his face toward Mannington. A sleepless night had wearied Ruxton and left a shadow on his thinking. He'd set a goal when he'd come to the Bootjack, and his feeling was strong that the goal was very near, so near that he was filled with impatience. Yet now, more than ever, he must be careful, damned careful. He could hear the clink of that twenty-five thousand dollars reward money, and it made sweet music in his ears.

Hang onto yourself, his instinct shouted, but still impatience tautened him.

Last night, when he'd stood in that ancient dugout and heard Laura Brownlee announce that Packrat Purdy had vanished, he'd taken the news without flinching. Not that it hadn't hit him hard. But often in a long career of

142

pursuing an easy dollar he'd been checkmated, and often he'd wrung a new chance out of disaster. "Torgin's found him," the girl had said, and that remark had pointed Ruxton's way. He'd been prepared to split the reward with Cole Manning, if necessary, though the notion had held no pleasure. But the trail had taken a sudden new turn and given Ruxton his chance to work alone again.

He'd known Torgin as a name belonging to a brand called Slash 7, and that was all he'd needed. His first day in Mannington, Ruxton had gone to the livery and rented the horse he now rode, and at the same time he'd got the hostler to draw him a detailed map of the Bootjack, a map showing the location of every landmark and every ranch, and he'd found out the name of each rancher and his brand. All this information Ruxton had memorized. No telling what small detail might serve him in good stead, as had that brief mention about Torgin last night.

After leaving the dugout, he'd gone to where he'd tied his horse. Before the dawn showed, he was scouting the vicinity of Slash 7. He might have missed

143

the trail leading down to the buildings except that he remembered the hostler's saying that Slash 7 was in a canyon. He'd gone part way down the trail until in the first light he could discern the roof tops below, and here he waited till morning crept into the canyon and he could make a careful study of Mack Torgin's place.

A poorly kept ranch, he decided, going to seed not for lack of money but because this Mack Torgin obviously didn't give a hoot for appearance. Even the few penned cattle that Ruxton saw looked sick. But he was not concerned with these matters, beyond what they might tell him about Torgin's personality; and they told him enough. He'd seen Torgin in Mannington the day before and inquired as to his identity and cataloged Torgin as a brute with just enough brains to get by. Slash 7 bore out that first impression. But what Slade Ruxton had sought in the blossoming dawn was the answers to two questions. Was Packrat Purdy a prisoner below? And if so, why?

Granting that the girl had been right in her surmise that Purdy had fallen into Slash 7's hands, what would Torgin have done with the oldster? Toted him back to jail? That would have been Torgin's natural move if his interest in Purdy were impersonal. And why had the Brownlee girl sensed that it was Torgin who'd found Purdy? Why not any of a dozen other ranchers in the Boot-jack? Ruxton's long, saturnine face puckered with puzzlement there on the canyon trail. Seemed Laura Brown-lee had reason to believe that Mack Torgin had some special interest in Packrat Purdy. Therefore she'd auto-matically thought of Torgin when Purdy had turned up missing. What, then, was that special interest? Something dating back to that twenty-four-year-old affair?

Now, Torgin was an old-timer in the basin. Ruxton had also learned that in Mannington yesterday. Give one of those town yokels a smile and a wide-eyed look like you considered him more important than President Taft and you could get an answer to anything, pro-vided you put the question so you didn't sound like you were plain nosy. And when you added one piece of informa-tion to another, you finally came out with an answer.

The Wells Fargo reward? Was that what interested Torgin? But Cole Manning hadn't seemed to know about the reward, and most people would likely have forgotten after twenty-four years. It was only the Slade Ruxtons who went after opportunity instead of waiting for it to knock, digging into dusty archives and old newspaper files for the hidden gold that was sometimes to be found. And so he pondered as he looked down upon Slash 7.

He watched the ranch come to life, men appearing sleepily from the bunkhouse to work the pump and wash before the cookshack door. Their voices rose to him in the clear air, and he became concerned lest he be spotted up here. Bushes grew along the trail, and he got down from his horse and dragged it to meager shelter. He felt safe enough then unless some sharp-eyed one happened to take a real look.

The cook appeared in his flour-sack apron to ring a bell; the crew hurried into the cookshack. Ruxton was sure he recognized the two who'd been with Torgin in town the day before. He became acutely conscious of hunger. He'd seen no sign of Torgin, and he kept his eyes on the big frame ranch house, waiting and hoping.

Then Torgin came from the house — no mistaking that big, blocky figure — and with him came a tall man whom Ruxton was certain he'd never seen before. Neither had he ever laid eyes on the stoop-shouldered figure between the two, but that was the one who really interested him. He'd wrangled a description of Packrat Purdy from the townspeople, and he'd have bet half the Wells Fargo money that the third man down there was Purdy.

The two were escorting Purdy to the cookshack, and their air was vigilant enough, even though Purdy didn't seem disposed to bolt. The oldster dragged his feet as he walked and looked as though he'd had a weary night of it. All this Slade Ruxton saw; and after the three disappeared into the cookshack, he still waited, having then the answer to the first of the two questions he'd asked himself. Packrat Purdy was indeed a prisoner of Slash 7.

In due course the crew spilled from the cookshack, Torgin with them, barking orders that lifted up to Ruxton, orders dealing with fence repairs and the other chores of the day. Then Torgin went back toward the ranch house, holding tightly to Purdy's arm. That tall, lean one who'd helped escort Purdy to the cookshack had gone to the corral and saddled up. Ruxton saw him ride across the yard and realized with faint alarm that the fellow was taking the trail that climbed up to the canyon's rim.

At once Ruxton scurried out of there and back to a clump of trees not far from the rim. He was in those trees and holding tight to his mount's nostrils when the tall, lean one rode so close by that Ruxton could almost have touched him. A hawk's face with a pair of pointed eyebrows. Blue eyes that were like ice. A hard one bent upon grim business. Ruxton would remember that fellow if he saw him again. The rider turned south and was soon lost from sight. Ruxton wondered what this man's mission might be and made his own shrewd guess.

Now that Slash 7 had Purdy, did they also want Laura Brownlee in the bag? The girl was down there to the south, in that dugout with Cole Manning, unless the two had decamped last night.

Ruxton wondered what a clash between Manning and Icy-Eyes would be like. They both had the look of being hard and quick, with a taste for violence in them. But he decided he'd put his betting money on Icy-Eyes, given the choice. The trouble with the Cole Mannings was that they ran around loaded down with ideals, and sometimes the load slowed them.

He thought of this as he rode toward Mannington, and he got the uncomfortable feeling that maybe his judgment was wrong. Studying on it, he knew with disconcerting certainty that Cole Manning was the real menace to any scheming he, Slade Ruxton, might do. You could find at least a little avarice in most men, and thus you could best them at the game, for you were the artisan of opportunity. The stumbling-block was one like Manning, who was your opposite and therefore often unfathomable.

But this factor mustn't grow to be any great concern. Right now he had a decision to make. It all added up to this. He had to get Purdy away from Slash 7, and he had to get Purdy to talk, to name that holdup man of long ago.

Whereupon the arrest could be made and the reward collected. Sometimes a situation arose when you had to count on local law whether you wanted to or not. That was the way things now shaped up.

He'd had Sheriff Burke Griffin pointed out to him in Mannington, but he'd swapped no words with the officer. A slow-witted one, that Griffin, for sure, a man fat in the body and fat in the head. Often you could sell these reuben star toters a fancy song and get them eating out of your hand. It had been Slade Ruxton's experience that most men could be tools if properly approached. But you had to be careful. He'd followed a number of careers in Montana this past decade, all of them of a kind to keep his hands soft, his mind sharp, and his pockets lined. But the misses were as frequent as the hits, no matter how cagey a person was. He'd been a land locater, and he'd manipulated mining stocks and promoted a town or two, and sometimes he'd reaped the rewards and sometimes he'd hopped the freight out, one jump ahead of the boys with the tar pots and the feather pillows.

This bounty-hunting was as chancy as any of the games he'd played. It gave you the backing of the law, and thus you didn't have to be afraid of a Cole Manning when you met up with one in the dark, like last night. But you had to watch that too many people didn't get their fingers in the pie. Like Sheriff Burke Griffin.

He sighted Griffin's town ahead and came across the bridge and into the main street, and as he passed the jail building, he saw the portly figure of Griffin in a chair on the sagging porch. He only lifted his hand to Griffin in passing, and he received a lazy salute in return. He rode on to the livery and put his horse away and, mindful of both his appearance and his hunger, chose to take care of his appearance first. A smell of talc always impressed these small-towners. Moreover, the barber had proved a font of knowledge when Ruxton had stopped in yesterday after-noon for a hair trim he hadn't needed.

Ruxton dropped into the chair a sec-ond time and ordered a shave. "Mack Torgin in town today?" he asked from the corner of his mouth as the lather was being laid on.

"Ain't seen him," the barber said gruffly.

Wariness at once touched Ruxton. Had it got around that he'd been asking too many questions without giving any information about himself? "I buy a few cattle once in a while," he said. "Heard Torgin might have some for sale."

"He might," the barber agreed, his voice a little friendlier.

Ruxton waited till the shaving was done and the cloth whisked away. Stepping to the mirror and adjusting his string tie, he willed his face to an expression of friendly conspiracy. "Look," he said then. "I'm a stranger and ripe for a fleecing. Here's a twenty-dollar bill to stave off my being swindled. All I want is the answer to a fair question. Is Torgin the kind to play a mite crooked?"

The barber looked at the greenback. "Go ask Doc Brownlee," he said.

"The man who runs the hospital? Why him?"

The barber took the bill. "It's whispered around that Torgin's been butchering some diseased beef. I ain't saying it's so, mind you. But talk has it that Brownlee may have to lower the ax on him. Doc's county health official." He folded the bill and tucked it away. "I don't hold with a man selling poisoned meat. The shave's on the house."

"Thanks," Ruxton said and moved out to the street.

He was very hungry, but he resolutely passed two restaurants on his way to the jail building. He'd delayed long enough, and impatience was beginning to ride him again; and besides, a man's brain was sharper when his stomach wasn't full. He walked along briskly until he reached the porch upon which Burke Griffin sat, idly fanning at flies. He looked at the immense man wedged down into his chair and hoped that his contempt for Griffin didn't show. He said affably, "My name is Ruxton, Sheriff. Slade Ruxton."

"I know," Burke Griffin said with equal affability. "You registered at the hotel the day before yesterday. You put down Denver as your address. You must have been absent-minded, mister. They never heard of you in Denver. I wired down there."

Ruxton stiffened, knowing just the faintest of fears. Now that had been a damn-fool thing, putting down Denver

153

so as to give the impression of being from out of state. But he smiled. "Then you also found that no police are looking for me. Why did you bother, Sheriff?"

Griffin waved his free hand in a lazy gesture that took in the entire street. "It's my town to law, and my county. When a stranger shows up, I like to have a line on him. If he's okay, no harm's done."

"Fair enough," Ruxton said, but he was now a wary man who'd made a false estimate of another and awakened to his error in time. His smile widened. "By the same token, you're entitled to the truth. I represent Wells Fargo. Care to see my credentials?"

"Ain't necessary," Griffin said. "You wouldn't be willing to show 'em if you didn't have 'em." He nodded toward the office behind him. "If you came about the jewelry from that old holdup, it's under lock and key. Like I told your San Francisco office when I made the checkup, it has to be held for a while as evidence."

"Till this man Purdy tells you the name of the highwayman?"

Griffin managed a shrug.

154

Ruxton leaned forward, raising one boot to the first step leading up to the porch. "What would you do, Sheriff, if I told you Purdy's present whereabouts?"

"I wouldn't get into any lather. Truth of it is, Mr. Ruxton, I don't believe Packrat can remember twenty-four years back."

"Then you're not really interested in arresting him?"

"He'll show up one of these days."

Ruxton said, very carefully, "Suppose he were being held prisoner at one of the ranches."

Griffin lost his affability. "Which ranch?" he demanded and almost came out of the chair. His face had turned the color of putty, and his hands made flailing movements. "Which ranch, damn you?"

Ruxton shook his head. "I don't feel that I should say until you've signified that you'll do something about it. Just what is your stand, really?"

Griffin sank back in his chair, and Ruxton could see that the man had hold of himself again.

Griffin's eyes squinted down. "Mister," he said, "I've been sheriff hereabouts for exactly twenty years. People like my

155

way of doing things enough to elect me again and again. I've talked to Wells Fargo people in the past on one case and another. I've talked to Pinkertons and private detectives in hard hats and buttoned shoes; and I've talked to federal marshals, and to sheriffs who'd strayed too far off their home ranges. I never found that I needed to take lessons from any of them or explain myself to them. I'm a little too old to change now."

Ruxton turned a cool face to him. "Then I think that I'll keep my findings to myself."

"You do that," Griffin said.

Ruxton brought his boot to the boardwalk with a thud, turned on his heel, and walked away, a high anger in him. He'd given more than he'd got; he'd pitted himself against this back-country sheriff and come off second best. That made a hard blow to vanity. But all the while he was cautioning himself, saying over and over in his mind, *Careful! Careful!* for the game was neither lost nor won, not yet.

He had learned only this — he couldn't count on Burke Griffin's being a tool to his hand. No, he'd learned more than that. Griffin pretended disinterest, but behind that pretense lay a real concern. He'd fetched Griffin one in the belly when he'd mentioned Purdy's being a prisoner.

So thinking, he came abreast of one of the restaurants, and its odors smote him heavily, and he turned inside. He took a table near the window and looked at the pencil-scrawled menu without any real interest. He gazed through the grimy glass and for the first time saw Burke Griffin out of his chair. The sheriff was cutting diagonally across the street, waddling swiftly toward the hospital; he disappeared inside. Ruxton's interest sharpened. In a few minutes Griffin reappeared at the hospital door, an old woman on crutches following him. The old woman stood talking to Griffin; the sheriff looked up and down the street, his round face perturbed.

A girl came to Ruxton's elbow to take his order. He gave it in an impatient voice, still watching through the window. If he could only hear what those two over there were talking about! Griffin waddled back toward the jail building and thus moved out of Ruxton's sight. The old woman still stood in the doorway of the hospital. She, too, was peering frantically along the street. Presently Dr. Brownlee showed, moving along the boardwalk, a portly, gray-haired man with dignity. The old woman hobbled out on her crutches to meet him; Ruxton watched her jabbering and gesticulating in the direction of the jail. Again he wished for ears sharp enough to overcome the barrier of wall and distance.

Now Brownlee reached and patted the old woman's shoulder reassuringly, though Brownlee had himself become agitated, if Ruxton were any judge. Brownlee stepped off the boardwalk and cut across the street, passing from Ruxton's vision.

The waitress was back again, placing a bowl of soup before him. He stared into its greasy depths, his mind busy, for he was remembering that scanty bit of information he'd got from the barber and trying to tie it in with the rest he'd learned. Brownlee — Torgin — Griffin — Purdy. Somehow they were all linked together, if a man could only get the full truth.

But Slade Ruxton had a closer concern. He'd tried to strike a bargain with Burke Griffin and failed. Now there was another with whom he must bargain, and so he must hit the saddle again as soon as he was fed and rested.

Chapter Ten

SUNDOWN

To Cole Manning, dropping down the canyon trail to Slash 7 in that same late afternoon, there had come the sense of loneliness from having left Laura behind; but he also knew a sharp wariness. He supposed this came in part from Laura's fears for him. Moreover, he'd cut out a sizable chunk of work for himself, what with Gal down below, and Torgin, too, neither of them any more eager to see him than they'd be to find a cactus in their boot. Damned if this wasn't a case of a boy going to do a man's chore. But something in that thought brought his pride rising, for he was reminded of his real mission in the Bootjack. On another day it might have been Flint Manning who rode this trail.

Thinking thus, he half regretted the security he'd gained by his arrangement with Laura that would have her scurrying for help if he didn't return by sundown. Better the danger than having to be fished from it.

Still, a man could get so brave that he died from bravery. He looked upon the roof tops below and saw the scattered buildings not as a ranch but as the stronghold of an enemy, and he began making a sharp study of Slash 7 and its surroundings, wanting to know all he might need to know if he were pressed hard. He even drew rein and lifted the field glasses from his saddlebag and got them to his eyes.

The canyon, he saw, was shaped like an arrowhead, with its far end a mere slot through which a creek flowed, willow-bordered and rollicking. Nearer, the canyon spread wide and stood hemmed by cliffs of rosy rock. Cottonwoods grew down there, serving as a windbreak and set out doubtless because the Homestead Law required this, and there were mountain birch and quaking aspen along the creek. The ranch itself seemed asleep, no man showing, and only a wisp of smoke rising lazy-like from the cookshack. He drew no surety from this seeming peacefulness. Spider webs were quiet, too.

He put the glasses away and dropped on down the trail, taking the switchbacks carefully and coming at last to the canyon's bottom.

The ranch yard spread before him in all its littered slovenliness, with the house gaunt and ugly just ahead and the sick cattle standing in the corral. You could take the measure of Mack Torgin by one look around this place. But the real thought in Manning was that he'd been here before, as a small boy. This was surprising, another of those lost shards of memory that suddenly glinted bright out of the obscurity of the years. He'd come with his father, and he'd heard talk between Flint Manning and Mack Torgin about some strays that had vanished from one of the other basin ranches. That was it.

Clear now was the remembrance of Torgin saying truculently, "Take a look around if you want," and a boy riding behind his father's saddle as they'd followed the canyon to its farther end. They'd found no strays, but Flint Manning hadn't really seemed to expect to, not that trip. Looking back across the twenty-two years, Cole Manning got the impression that it had just been a routine checkup his father had made. They'd turned it into quite a holiday;

162

they'd dug for Indian arrowheads at the foot of a cliff and found a few, along with some discarded bits of obsidian. His father had shown him a ring of tepee stones and told him how the Indians had lived in the Bootjack not so many years before and made camp at this very spot.

And again Mack Torgin stood in his doorway, big and blocky and black-browed, looking as truculent as he had that other visit. It was as if he, Cole Manning, had grown up but time had stood still for Torgin while one day had worked itself around a long circle to blend into another.

Stepping down from his saddle unbidden, Manning said, "Howdy, Mack."

There was no more welcome in Torgin than there was juice in a boiled boot, and there was no surprise in him, either. He said, "I figured that sooner or later you'd find your way down the trail," and he put such bluster into it that it struck Manning that Torgin was afraid.

Thus was the first victory Manning's, but it made him no less wary. He looked at Torgin and was again reminded of a grizzly bear. One poke with the stick and you'd have Torgin rampaging. Around them the ranch dreamed in the last of the day, and out of the willows bordering the creek came four riders, heading toward the corrals. They rode in slowly, not looking primed for trouble. Manning took his eyes from Torgin long enough to be sure that none of these was Gal.

Torgin asked, "Well, what do you want?"

Manning shrugged. "Were you expecting me because you've got a couple of people who don't belong here?"

"A couple?" Torgin repeated and his face showed true surprise.

"One called Gal, though he's down on the book as Texas Joe Bridger, late of Deer Lodge. There's a law against going over the wall. And there's a law for those that keep a convict in hiding afterward."

Torgin said, "Well, I'll be damned!"

He'd been hit hard, as Manning could plainly see. Torgin hadn't expected anybody would be looking for Gal. It was Packrat Purdy who was on his brutish mind, and this sudden shift had caught him off balance. Manning knew a certain delight, though he kept himself still-faced.

"How about it?" he asked.

Torgin's eyes squinted down. "Maybe he didn't tell me about his back trail." He opened and closed his broad hands. "You can't pin this on me," he said, making it blustery, too blustery, and Manning thought, *He'd throw his right-hand man to me if it meant saving his own skin. He's got no more loyalty than a louse, and no more guts,* though he wasn't sure about the last part of his estimate.

He said, "I'm here for a look around."

"Look all you want," Torgin said, like an echo out of the lost past when Cole Manning had ridden here with his father.

Those four were down from leather and off-saddling out there by the corral; and Torgin looked toward them, his face showing nothing, his eyes only slightly speculative. They stared back at their boss, and Torgin shook his head ever so slightly, but the tension mounted in Manning.

He stood with the reins lax in his hands; he stood indolent, but he was fixing the pattern of the yard in his mind, and there was mighty little shelter near where he stood. He could make a lunge

165

for the Winchester in its saddle scabbard, but one rifle wouldn't add up to five Colts. Let something uncork, and his best bet was to rush Torgin and bowl him over and so gain the shelter of the house. Torgin looked soft around the middle and a hard belting might drive him down. But he mustn't make that play until the real need arose. He mustn't lose the edge he'd gained, and that edge was Torgin's fear.

He said softly, "Mack, I've got a marshal's badge pinned under my vest."

"I know that," Torgin said. "I recognized you the first day, and I can still read newspaper print if I put on a pair of cheaters. How do you fit this into a federal case?"

"Turning Gal over to the warden would be just a service to the state," Manning admitted. "It's Packrat Purdy I'm really after. If it's legality you're questioning, there was mail lifted in that stagecoach robbery years back."

"Look all you want," Torgin said again.

Manning nodded. "I'll do that."

Those four had finished unsaddling and were now washing up at the pump. All but one, who'd already finished and moved to the bench before the cookshack. Manning looked at the lowering sun. A little early for supper. The man on the bench had his hat slanted low over his eyes and a hard jaw showing below. He stared fixedly at Manning. One of those who'd got spilled by a taut rope in a cottonwood clump and still nursed his anger? Manning wasn't sure. He turned a shoulder to the man and, leading his horse, headed toward the barn.

Torgin came along, limping slightly. Manning fell back a pace and let Torgin come abreast of him. Inside the barn, Manning tied his sorrel in an empty stall and prowled the gloomy depths. He had a peek into the harness room. He climbed to the loft and peered into its far corners. When he came down the ladder, Torgin was awaiting him, a dim figure in the semigloom; but he could see Torgin's smile.

Anger touched Manning like a passing wind. "You can save me time," he said. "Where are you keeping him?"

Torgin's smile broadened. "What good would it do to tell you he ain't on Slash 7?"

Manning strode out of the barn. Two more horsemen had ridden in, but neither was Gal. These paid no heed to Manning, though he passed close to the pair as he cut over to the bunkhouse. En route, he skirted the corral with the sick cattle and was reminded of the talk between Torgin and Doc Brownlee in the hospital. His surety blossomed again; Purdy *had* to be here.

He got to the bunkhouse and had only to lean through the door to have a complete look. The place was as untidy as he'd supposed it would be, the blankets a tangle and the table cluttered with playing-cards and poker chips, and the floor looking as though it hadn't known a scrub brush for a month of Sundays. No one was here.

Torgin, close beside him, said, "Convinced yet?"

Manning went next to the cookshack. The cook, who was setting the table, turned a truculent face to the intruder. Manning went along the room to have a look into the kitchen. It was empty. He moved far enough into the kitchen to be sure of that. He went to each of the various outbuildings and stood at last before the open door of the blacksmith shop. It was getting on toward sundown, for he'd spent a good half hour at the search, and now there were more horses than before in the corral, and he'd lost count of the number of riders who'd drifted in. A half dozen sat before the cookshack; others moved in the yard.

Torgin said, "You forgot to look in the root cellar."

"Where is it?"

"Behind the house."

"Show me," Manning said.

The root cellar was a small dirt-roofed dugout with a heavy door. Manning climbed down and peered into the darkness beyond the door, a darkness rank with the smell of vegetables stored here through the long, hard Bootjack winters. He was sure no one would be here; Torgin had been too eager to point out the place. Still, he scratched a match to life for a real look. Then he shut the door.

"Satisfied?" Torgin asked.

"There's still the house, Mack."

Torgin sighed. "Come along," he said, and led the way around to the front door. The parlor seemed big and gloomy, and Torgin at once got a lamp burning. His face showed blocky and fathomless when the light touched it;

the humor he'd found in Manning's futile search was gone. He adjusted the wick to his satisfaction, then spread his hands in a wide gesture. "Look around all you like."

In Manning a sense of defeat took hold. Torgin's continued willingness to have Slash 7 searched indicated that the house held no secret. Yet Purdy had vanished from that coulee dugout, and the sign said that Purdy had been carried away by a horseman. By some honest rancher who'd since lodged Purdy in the Mannington jail? What a laughingstock Flint Manning's son would be if he continued pushing a search for a man who was already behind bars!

Someone raised a call out in the yard, high-pitched and meaningless; a dog barked. Manning got a feeling of being surrounded, and a feeling that time was running out. There was light at the windows, and the lamp wasn't really needed, not yet. How the blazes did you tell when it was sundown in mountain country? Up along the Marias, the sun dropped off the edge of the earth, but in the Bootjack it was sundown in one place sooner than in another.

Maybe Laura was already on her way to Mannington for help. This thought rankled in him. Flint Manning hadn't needed any posse to back him; even on the Marias, shed of a badge, he'd chosen to go after Texas Joe Bridger alone.

"Where does that door lead?" Manning asked, indicating one in the parlor wall.

"A closet." Torgin moved to the fireplace woodpile and dug from it a whisky bottle. He turned and said in his deep voice, "Sit down and have a drink. You're like a dog chasing his tail, kid. You'll never catch up with it. Sit down, I say. Care to hear the Graphophone? I've got a bunch of those *Uncle Josh* records. Funniest damn things you ever heard. You might as well make the rest of your stay a friendly call." But the voice wasn't friendly.

Manning shook his head. "There's still Gal."

"He took off this morning on a *pasear* of his own. Matter of fact, he's been hunting you. Doesn't like anyone named Manning. He finally told me so." He held up the whisky bottle and swished its contents. "How about a drink?"

"Have one yourself," Manning said.

In the next ten minutes he put his nose into every ground-floor room, seeing the filthy kitchen and the cubbyhole where Torgin slept and another bedroom that probably hadn't been used for months. Manning could have traced his name in the dust of the window sill.

He came back to find Torgin seated on a straight-backed chair near that closed door Manning had asked about. Torgin had taken a pull at the bottle and was drawing his sleeve across his mouth. He looked bolder and easy in his mind. He looked like a bear in honey season. He grinned at Manning and made a gesture of offering the bottle.

"Got a cellar in this place?" Manning asked.

Torgin shook his head. "The root cellar was dug before the house went up. It made cellar enough."

"How do I get upstairs?"

Torgin's face tightened, and his eyes shone pale. "The upstairs was closed off four winters back. No sense in heating it, and no need to open it since. Man, haven't you caught on yet that nobody's hid here?"

"Just the same, I'll have a look."

Hoofbeats beat hard in the yard, and

expectancy came into Torgin's eyes. He stood up abruptly and strode toward the front door. Yanking it open, he had a look outside, peering hard. "Who's that?" he called, and Manning heard the answer come across the reach of the yard. "It's Charley, Mack." Torgin closed the door and moved the full width of the room to that straight-backed chair and carefully seated himself again. By that door. It seemed to Manning that the room had turned close and stuffy, with something electric in the air.

He said, "The upstairs, remember? I'll have a look."

Torgin scowled. "Now that's a damn-fool notion."

The supper bell sounded, clear and mellow and almost in the room. Torgin stood up from the chair, still holding the bottle. "You might as well eat, long as you're here. Let's go and put our feet under the table."

There it was again, the friendly offer without the friendly voice, and now Manning understood. Plain as hoofprints in the dust. Torgin had been willing enough to let him look every-where, not balking until upstairs had been mentioned. Torgin had been bluffing and hadn't been too bright about it at that, showing ease the longer they kept away from the house, even reminding Manning of the root cellar, but getting edgy at the last. And all this while, Torgin had been buying time. Time for Gal to come riding back to Slash 7. Time for Gal to get here and face up to a Manning.

No wonder Torgin had jumped so fast when that last rider had ridden up; only the rider had turned out to be someone named Charley. And there were other signs that pointed to the truth. Torgin had chosen a straight-backed chair in preference to the rockers here in the parlor and walked the width of the room to get back to that particular chair. The chair by the door.

And because all these things made a pattern, Manning darted quickly to that door and wrenched it open and saw a stairs before him.

Torgin exploded then, and Manning had a quick remembrance of thinking how one poke with a stick could start a grizzly rampaging. Torgin came off the chair, swinging the whisky bottle at Manning's head. Manning pulled his head aside and lunged at Torgin. He could almost see the shout that was rising in Torgin's throat, and he wondered if it would carry to the cookshack where the crew was now assembling. He couldn't risk that.

He struck out with his left fist and caught Torgin in the midriff. Fat there, all right — too much fat. Torgin's breath went out of him; he stumbled and went down on one knee, but he let go of the whisky bottle and wrapped his arms around Manning's legs and brought Manning down, too. Manning writhed free and got a stand and started for the stairs.

Only dimly did he hear the front door bang open. That far corner was in shadow with the horn of the Graphophone glimmering faintly, but he got a hazy glimpse of two figures. "Hold it!" someone cried, and he knew that voice to be Gal's. But it was Laura Brownlee who was screaming, "Cole! Watch out!"

Now Manning saw Gal move into the room, into the light, a gun in his right hand, the fingers of his left closed around Laura's wrist. Gal's eyes found Manning and impaled him. Torgin, on the floor, let out a throaty roar that held triumph. Manning thought of his gun and fought down a heady impulse to try for it. There was just enough coolness left in him to know that Laura would be standing in the way of the shooting.

Chapter Eleven

GUNS AT SLASH 7

Torgin drew his knees up under him and lurched to a clumsy stand; his boot struck the fallen whisky bottle and sent it rolling across the floor. He was breathing hard. He got to Manning and jerked the forty-five from Manning's holster and sent the gun sailing in the direction of the fireplace. The gun hit and fell, making a great clatter. Torgin said in a wheezy voice, "That fixes him, Gal. That draws his fangs. God, I thought you'd never get here!"

Gal stepped sideways into the room, pulling Laura along; he flung her into one of the rawhide-bottomed rockers, not being mean about it, saying absently, "Behave yourself, girl," as though he really didn't know she was on earth. He still had his eyes fixed on Manning; his eyes were a cold-blue blaze, and in Manning rose the realization that this was the most dangerous moment he'd known in the Bootjack. Coupled with that was a deep disappointment at the way the hand had played out; another ten minutes might have made all the difference, getting him up those stairs and back down again, Purdy in tow. Now he felt itchy in the knuckles but impotent. He felt pinned down.

Torgin said, "How did you come by her?" jerking his head toward Laura. She sat deep in the chair, her eyes wide and luminous but not showing any panic.

"I was riding back from the basin," Gal said tonelessly, his eyes never leaving Manning. "She was hanging around up on the rim. Yesterday I let her get away. This time I brought her in." Then, nodding stiffly toward Manning, he said with fierce intensity, "Give him back his gun, Mack."

Torgin said, startled, "You crazy?"

"Give him back his gun!"

"Man, this is Slash 7, not the middle of Bootjack Basin!"

"Once before you thought it wasn't the time or place," Gal said, his face stony and only his voice alive. "He's not going to slip away again. Damn it, why do you think I've ridden a horse half to death these last couple of days?"

Triumph's first flush had passed from Torgin, and now he was a worried man

178

in the lamplight. His broad face showed this; he was beyond bluster; he'd had time to begin to think, and the tone he used on Gal was almost pleading. "We're on thin ice, you and me," he said. "Unless Purdy names the man I think he will, we're jail bait for fair. Don't you understand? We've got to make Purdy talk before we can do a thing. No two ways about it. I'd have got the truth out of him last night if you hadn't balked at the rough stuff. Remember that, Gal."

"I fetched him here because you wanted him," Gal said. "That didn't mean I was willing to stand by and see fire put to an old man's feet. But that's got nothing to do with what we're talking about."

"It's got everything to do with it," Torgin insisted. He was sweating a little; he dragged a bandanna from his hip pocket and mopped his forehead. "It's all tied together, Gal. You bought into my game when you came here; I bought into yours when I let you stay, knowing" — he shot a cautious glance at Manning — "what I did about your back trail. If Purdy tells me the right name, I can ride high and handsome in this basin.

But right now I'm in a split stick, and you want to wedge me tighter. That's what it adds up to. Start gunplay in this room and probably both of us will look up a rope in a gallows yard. I didn't bargain for that when I took you in, Gal."

The fire burned less brightly in Gal's eyes. He looked like a man making a hard fight with himself. "I didn't think about it that way." he said. "What do you want to do?"

Manning stared in surprise, seeing Gal swerved thus. *He's loyal,* Manning thought and found this almost a paradox until he remembered that Gal had been a cowboy. *He's loyal, and as much as he hates me, he'll remember that loyalty first.* But he knew this notion held a false hope, for the wildness that showed on Gal could only be kept so long in leash.

Laura said, from the chair, "I'm sorry, Cole. He came up as quiet as smoke. He'd grabbed me before I knew he was around. Some watchdog I made!"

Manning said gently, "Never mind," yet his real concern was for her.

Torgin drew his heavy brows together. "What do I want to do? I say let's wrap

180

these two up and put them somewhere till we make Purdy talk." He walked to the whisky bottle, picked it up, and had a pull at it. He nearly used up the whisky with that one swig. He offered the bottle to Gal, who shook his head. Torgin crossed over to the fireplace woodpile, and buried the bottle deep. "That's it, we'll put 'em away."

"Upstairs?" Gal asked, nodding toward the door Manning had wrenched open.

Torgin shook his head. "Let Purdy see friends around and he might get braver. No, the root cellar, I think." He lifted his gun from leather and waggled it in a wide arc that swept from Manning to Laura and back again. "Come on, you two," he said. "We're going for a walk. Gal, there's a lantern in the kitchen. Fetch it along."

Manning said, "Think twice, Mack. Have you forgot about my badge? You've showed yourself leery of the law. Are you leery enough?"

Torgin's eyes turned scared, but he made his voice bold. "Another night may make a heap of difference."

Gal had moved toward the kitchen; he came back holding an unlighted lantern. Laura wearily arose, and she and Manning were herded out of the house ahead of the two men. Now it was truly sundown, with the yard twilit gray and the afterglow tingeing the canyon's rim and all things losing shape. Lamplight glowed in the bunkhouse, and from the sounds that came through its open door, Manning judged that a poker game was under way. Gal's horse stood ground-anchored before the ranch house, and Laura's unsaddled mount was tied near by. Wordlessly Gal lifted a lariat from his saddle and hung the coiled rope over his arm.

Behind Manning, Torgin said, "Around this way," and Manning felt the prod of a gun barrel. He glanced at Laura; her lips were drawn tight, but her chin was steady.

They came around the house to the root cellar and were urged down the steps. Now Gal lighted the lantern and held it high as Torgin put his shoulder to the door. Beyond, Manning saw heaped potatoes. Two peeled poles, spaced perhaps six feet apart, supported the dirt roof of the cellar. Torgin said with satisfaction, "Tie the two of them so they won't be able to work on

182

each other. Here, do you need a jack-knife?"

But Gal was already busy cutting the rope in two. He came behind Manning, jerked at his arms and pulled them together. Manning felt the hemp tighten around his wrists. He was hauled roughly to one of the supporting poles and lashed there, tied low so that he could sit on the earth floor with his back to the pole. He saw Laura trussed to the other upright in similar fashion. She made no protest.

Torgin picked up the lantern and held it high, inspecting Gal's work. Torgin's face showed satisfaction. "They'll keep," he decided.

Manning said, "You might bring us something to eat."

Torgin grunted. Gal said, "Sure." His eyes showed icy-blue in the lantern light; when he looked at Manning, the hate was so strong in him as to be almost tangible.

Torgin said, "Now let's go and have another talk with old Packrat." Irritation edged his voice. "Damn it, Gal, we'll get no place treating him gentle."

"He'll wear down," Gal said. "If you want to use him rough, you'll have to

183

turn him loose first and grab onto him all by yourself. Even so, there's some things I won't stomach. Haven't I made that clear yet?"

Torgin held the lantern to light Gal's footsteps from the dugout, then followed after the Texan, pulling the door shut behind them. At once Laura and Manning were smothered in darkness thick as soot. The boots of the departing two beat against the steps; the sound dwindled to nothing. In here was a tomb's silence, clammy and tense.

Out of the darkness, Laura said in a level voice, "What a queer mixture that man Gal is. So he's the one who carried off Packrat. Imagine his not wanting force used against Packrat lest it be on his conscience. Yet there's murder in him; it shows whenever he looks at you. Why is that, Cole?"

Manning shrugged. "Because Flint Manning put him in Deer Lodge for life. That was a long time ago. He hated Flint, so now he hates me. The warden warned me in that letter I was reading this morning."

They were both silent then. Manning strained his ears, trying to pick some translatable sound from the world beyond this makeshift prison. For a moment he thought he heard the scratchy, distant voice of the Graphophone, but he couldn't be sure. He had a sense of timelessness and a strangled feeling of being buried alive. When he spoke again, it was as much to hear his own voice and Laura's as for any other reason. Yet the question was vital enough. "Laura, is there anything you could tell me that might help us get out of this tight? Anything about what Packrat Purdy knows? I see now it's that old case Torgin's interested in."

She sighed. "Nothing would be changed."

Impatience rose in him; he'd grown tired of battling against that invisible wall. "How can you be sure?"

She said nothing for a long moment. Then: "Cole, try to believe this. It might be as much for your own sake as anyone's that the secret be kept."

He said angrily, "Riddles! Always riddles!"

She said, "Whatever happens now depends on Gal and Torgin. We've got Gal bucking Torgin about Packrat, but we've got Torgin growing more desperate. I've known him all my life, Cole.

He's on thin ice, and he's afraid. The trouble is, the more desperate Torgin gets, the more dangerous he'll become. Mark my word."

"But if I only knew what it is he hopes to wring out of Purdy."

"Shhh!" she said. "Someone's coming."

Boots sounded on the steps, and the door was thrust inward. Lantern light flashed against Manning's eyes, blinding him; the lantern was lowered to the cellar floor, and he saw the high stand of a man and recognized the fellow as the cook he'd seen so briefly when he'd inspected cookshack and kitchen. The cook carried a kettle.

"Stew," he said. He had a forty-five thrust into the band of his apron. Very carefully he untied Laura. "You eat," he ordered. "Then you feed him. I'm not taking any chances on turning him loose."

Laura rubbed her wrists. She lifted a large spoon from the kettle, dipped it, and offered a mouthful to Cole. Thus they ate, taking turns, the cook squatting down on his haunches and watching them closely, his face wooden. At last Laura asked, "Had enough?"

"Yes," Manning said. "For Pete's sake,

will you wipe off my chin?"

The cook said, "Get your back to that pole again, girl," and when Laura obeyed, he began working with the rope. He took his time at the task.

Manning studied the fellow, noting the dull face with its drooping mustache and empty eyes. Manning said, "I'd like to strike a bargain with you, friend."

The cook shook his head.

"Save your breath," Laura advised. "He's been on Slash 7 for at least twenty years. Torgin keeps him in whisky, and he keeps the spread in meals."

Some shadow of a pride once owned crossed the cook's lantern-lighted face. "I'm a mighty good cook."

"That was good stew," Laura said.

"Why, thank you kindly," the cook said, surprised.

He inspected the knots, picked up the lantern and the almost-emptied kettle, and clumped out of the place. The door closed again, and darkness and silence pressed down. Manning felt better for having eaten. He began working at the knots, yanking his wrists this way and that; but Gal had done a good job. A mighty good job indeed. Still Manning worked until he grew weary. His shoulders ached and his wrists were sore. He asked, "Do you think you could sleep?"

Laura answered drowsily, "I was just dozing off."

"I'm sorry," he said.

After that he kept silent. He listened to Laura's even breathing and finally decided that she had indeed fallen asleep. He tried sleeping himself, knowing he might need to be rested for whatever was to come. If he dozed, it was only fitfully, and he couldn't be sure that he ever quite edged beyond consciousness. He wondered how much time had elapsed since the cook had gone and couldn't be sure whether it was twenty minutes or several hours. He grew fretful and put his mind against his impatience, knowing it did him no good.

He thought, *A week in here would be like a year.* He began picturing his Marias ranch just to give himself something to think about, but dreaming of broad acres and rough river breaks and all that eternity of land stretching on up into Canada didn't make this root cellar any broader or the darkness less thick. More than that, he got to fretting about the ranch, wondering if he'd be back in time for fall roundup, wondering how his crew fared these days.

Was it midnight, he asked himself. Was it morning? No, not morning, for he could glimpse a bit of sky through an air vent overhead, but that air vent was roofed to keep the rain out and he couldn't even be sure there was moonlight. Darkness there; darkness here; darkness everywhere.

And a step on the stairs.

The door thrust inward, but no lantern light showed. Beyond the door was the night, moonlit, he saw now, but unattainable, blocked by the high silhouette of a man. Laura came awake and asked sleepily, "Who's that?" and Gal's soft voice spoke, probing the cellar. "Manning?"

In Manning rose the thought that something had changed, that Purdy had talked or Torgin's fear of holding a lawman prisoner had grown big enough to swallow the man, and thus Gal was here. But Manning's instinct told him that no such business had brought Gal, and so fear stirred deep in his belly, for hatred stood strong in that single inquiring call; and he had nothing to put

189

against Gal's hatred, not even his bare hands. Gal groped forward in the darkness, and the surprising thing was that he kneeled and fumbled at the knots, and shortly Manning felt himself freed. At first he merely sat, not comprehending what was expected of him.

"Stand up," Gal ordered.

Manning did so, his stirred blood like needles shuttling through him. This was like being drunk and finding you got no obedience from your legs. He rubbed at his wrists and was aware of Gal's nearness. He wondered if he could find the man's jaw in the darkness, and he made a fist out of his right hand, but his hand felt feathery.

"Outside," Gal said.

Manning stepped toward the door. "What about Laura?"

"She'll keep," Gal said. "Outside."

Manning shrugged. Somewhere in all this might lie a chance, but the chance had not yet shaped up. He moved through the open door and climbed the steps and stood in the night. He breathed deeply. The moon rode high enough to tell him it was past midnight, and the ranch lay ghostly. Bunkhouse and cookshack were shadow-swatched;

only a single light burned in the ranch house, in one of the upstairs rooms. The room where Purdy was held? Manning fell to figuring out the position of that room in proximity to the stairs.

Gal came close behind him. Manning felt a tug at his empty holster as a gun was dropped into it. Gal said, "It's your own. Keep your hand away from it. It hasn't any shells; I'll let you load later."

Manning supposed his surprise showed. "Why this?"

Gal stood high-shouldered in the moonlight, his face a silvery mask. "I've walked the yard till I've nearly worn out my boots. I've thought it over from every angle, and there's only one way. The two of us ride into the basin tonight, Manning. Somewhere we'll have it out, gun to gun."

Manning said, "So you've found a way to satisfy yourself without tangling Torgin into it. But still you're only half smart, Gal. What will any part of this game get you? You could turn around and cut Laura loose, too. The law would remember that."

Gal said, "How did you like it in the dark, mister, with the walls crowding you? How would you have liked it for

191

thousands of nights? Now do you understand what one Manning did to me?"

Manning shook his head. "You pack a hate a long time, mister."

"There's more to it than you know," Gal said. "The rest I'll tell you when I've let you load that gun." He walked forward a few paces ahead of Manning. He looked back. "Hurry up. I've got horses saddled and waiting."

Manning said, "I'd like to oblige you — " but again he was remembering Laura. He looked up at that one glowing window in the ranch house and knew that whatever chance could be made from this madness of Gal's would have to be fashioned here and now. He snatched his empty gun out then and hurled it straight at Gal's head. Pity stirred in Manning, and a certain remorse that such an act was necessary.

He saw the man go down, and he ran forward across the short distance between them and looked at the crumpled figure. Blood showed on Gal's temple where the skin had been broken, and blood trickled along Gal's lean jaw. The consciousness had gone out of the man, but not the hate; it was there still on the fixed face.

Chapter Twelve

ALARM IN THE NIGHT

He kneeled and lifted Gal's gun from its holster, but with the weapon in his hand, he didn't know what to do with it; so he flung it far out into the night. He picked up his own gun and plucked shells from his belt and quickly loaded, his mind racing every which direction trying to make capital from this turn of events that had left him a free man in the moonlight. He looked again toward the ranch house; that one upstairs light had winked out.

This startled him; his first thought was that some sound had reached the house and Torgin had doused the lamp, the better to peer from the window and study the night. Manning stared until his eyes hurt; he felt sweat on his palms. He tried to make himself small, a hard one to find. Then a new light blossomed, downstairs. He knew that room; he had inspected it when he'd searched the lower house. It was Torgin's bedroom.

He turned and darted back to the root

cellar and felt his way down the steps and put his shoulder against the door. He came into the darkness; and knowing what Laura's fear would be, he said quickly, "It's me — Cole." He groped to her and began working at the rope. He was wooden-fingered, slow at the job, and the knots were stubborn. He felt in his pockets for his jackknife, then remembered that the last time he'd used it he'd put it in his saddlebag.

Laura asked, "What happened?"

He made it short. "He wanted a chance at me, gun to gun. He cut me loose to get that chance. Alter he gave me my gun, I clouted him with it."

"Too bad you had to, Cole."

He said, "Some day I'll stand up to him. I couldn't afford it tonight."

She said thoughtfully, "Because of me, I suppose. Aren't you just as crazy as Gal in your own special way? Flint Manning was the one Gal really hated, so you think you've got to step into your father's boots. Where's the sense in that?"

"I've got to get you out of here," he said brusquely.

"And is that the only reason why you swallowed your pride and side-stepped a fight? I suppose I should thank you."

194

"Never mind," he said. "There — " The last knot came loose and he helped her to a stand. In the darkness she was warm against him; she filled his arms, she was softness in his arms. "Don't try walking till you're sure you can," he said. He began rubbing her wrists.

After a couple of minutes, she said, "I think I can make it."

They came out of the cellar together, Manning half supporting her. He saw at once that the light was gone from Torgin's bedroom and that Gal still lay crumpled upon the ground. He walked toward the fallen man and bent low for a look. His mind was racing again; he supposed he should drag Gal into the cellar and truss him up and thus make sure that Gal wouldn't rouse to spread the alarm before he and Laura were free of Slash 7. But the minutes seemed very precious now; and Gal looked like he was in for a long sleep. Remembering what Gal had said, Manning nudged Laura's elbow, heading her toward the house. "He's got horses saddled."

When they came around the building to its front yard, the horses were there, Manning's own and Gal's, and over by the fence a third unsaddled one. It was Laura's horse, left tied here since Gal had fetched her down from the rim.

Manning said exultantly, "He sure smoothed out the wrinkles for us. Lead your horse to where the canyon trail begins and don't mount till you're sure you're beyond earshot." His voice sounded loud in the stillness, and he dropped it a pitch. "Once you're up on the rim, gallop hard to Mannington."

"And you, Cole?"

"I'm going to get Purdy out of the house."

"Then I'll wait here for you."

"No!" he said and grew angry with her. He got his hands on her shoulders and shook her. He spoke louder than he intended. "It will be risky enough without my having to worry about you! Will you do as you're told?"

"I'll wait up on the rim for you, Cole. If there's any fuss down here, the sound will reach me."

"Get going, then," he said. "And take it easy till you're in the clear. They keep a dog on the place. He must be in the barn, or he'd be nosing around here by now. Watch yourself."

"I will."

She moved toward the unsaddled horse and untied the mount and led it through the gate. In the moonlight he watched her trim, almost boyish figure until she was a good hundred yards away, heading toward the canyon wall.

He moved quietly toward the door then and put his hand to the latch. Thank the stars that Montana ranchers didn't usually lock their houses! He let himself into the darkened parlor, and at once every piece of furniture was a hazard. A man would raise a terrible clatter if he bumped into that Graphophone. He paused here, recalling how this room had looked by lamplight. He heard a faint snoring near by and judged that Torgin was asleep. He breathed easier.

He got one hand against the wall and groped along it toward that door that gave to the stairs. He took each step carefully, but in spite of that he stumbled against a chair — that blasted straight-backed chair upon which Torgin had perched to guard the stairs that afternoon.

The snoring ceased. Manning froze where he stood, sure that the thundering of his heart must be reaching throughout the house. Torgin, in that not-too-distant bedroom, mumbled sleepily; bedsprings creaked. Was the man getting up, or was he merely turning over? Manning eased his gun from its holster and held it in his hand. Silence — a long sweep of silence. And then Torgin's snoring commenced anew.

Manning let himself through the doorway and put his foot to the stairs.

Those steps creaked so that it took him an eternity to make the ascent, and he was tempted to remove his boots. He gained the top and found himself in a hallway as dark as the root cellar had been. He groped along; there seemed to be a dozen doors giving off this hallway, but most of them proved to be open. The upstairs was musty and smelled of disuse and the droppings of mice. His eyes were growing used to the darkness. He figured out where that lighted window had been located when he'd viewed it from the outside and finally found the door that, by his judgment, had to be the right one. He turned the knob carefully and put pressure against it, but the door didn't give. Locked! His mind raced again; to slam his shoulder against the door would be to bring Torgin from his bed.

Then he fumbled below the knob. The key was there. Exultant again, he turned the key and eased the door inward. Its hinges protested, and a querulous voice demanded, "Who's there?"

"Shhhh!" Manning said in a quick, harsh whisper. "I'm a friend."

He risked a match, scraping it across his leathered thigh and holding it aloft. This room was bare of furniture, and upon a tangle of blankets in a far corner sat a shaggy-haired, vacuous-faced oldster who blinked at him. This, he knew, was Packrat Purdy; and Purdy said, "By grab, it's Flint! Long time no see, *amigo*. You come to get me out of this rat's nest?"

Flint? Manning got it then; this addled old fellow had noticed the resemblance and made no allowance for time. Manning asked, "You able to walk?"

"Could jig, for that matter. Torgin did a lot of jawing at me tonight and cuffed me a few times, but he didn't get nowheres near as rough as he'd 'a' liked. He's scared stiff of that jigger with the icy eyes. Me, too, Flint, and no denying it. But don't you worry. I didn't tell 'em a thing. Not a thing."

The match burned out. Manning said, "We've got to get out of here, Purdy, and we've got to be mighty quiet about it."

"Quiet as mice. Hee, hee! And glad to go along. The grub's kinda skimpy in these parts. Just a minute till I get my boots on."

Manning lighted another match and held it till Purdy was out of the room and to the head of the stairs. Purdy seemed spry enough, he noticed. He was right behind the old eccentric as they groped downward as quietly as they could. In the darkness of the parlor, Manning got a grip on Purdy's arm and whispered in his ear. "Mind the furniture," Manning warned. From that yonder bedroom, Torgin's snoring still rose. "This way, Purdy. The front door is straight ahead."

"Haze me along, Flint. I'm one old mossy-horn as is eager to see starlight."

"Here," Manning said a few breathless moments later. He groped for the latch. "I've got horses just outside."

And then the gun sounded. The gun spoke out in the yard. *God!* he thought. *Laura! Have you got safe away, Laura?*

That gun was a waspish one, not deep-throated like a Colt or a Winchester. About .22 caliber, Manning judged. It sounded once, it sounded again; and it was hard to place the sound, though it seemed to come from behind the house. Gal? But he'd flung Gal's gun away, and it had been a forty-five, at that. Then he understood, for he'd sensed that first day in the basin that Gal carried a hide-out gun; but he'd forgotten it tonight. A derringer, likely — he'd once seen a two-shot superimposed barrel model of Wesson make, and that might be the kind Gal was carrying. And Gal might readily have picked up such a gun in a secondhand store since leaving prison.

Now why hadn't he taken the extra few minutes to drag Gal into the root cellar and tie him? But the alarm was given. Inside the house, Torgin was roaring in the darkness, and someone raised a bellow in the bunkhouse. Manning propelled Purdy forward with a stiff, outthrust arm.

"Into saddle!" Manning shouted.

Out in the barn, the dog was barking furiously. He must have been shut in for the night, and he was lunging against the barn door. Lamplight sprang up in the bunkhouse. Someone, underwear-clad and looking like a wraith, showed in the bunkhouse doorway.

Manning was across the yard and lifting himself to his own saddle. Purdy snatched up the reins of Gal's cayuse and made an awkward attempt to mount. The horse shied, side-stepping and rolling its eyes. Purdy followed the mount in its skittish maneuvering. In Manning was the cry: *Hurry! Hurry!* but he made no sound. Purdy made a mighty effort and got up into leather. Gal's mount pitched a couple of times and swapped ends. Purdy jostled like a sack of grain and looked as though he might pitch over the horse's head. But he got the mount wheeled around.

They cut out through the gateway. Manning forced his horse parallel to the fence and looked in the direction of the root cellar, though the house blocked his view. He made out dim movement in the shadows by the house. For a moment he thought he was seeing an animal and wondered if the dog had freed himself from the barn. But an excited dog wouldn't move so slowly.

Then he recognized Gal, down on his hands and knees, crawling. And even as Manning watched, the strength went out of Gal and the man flattened to the ground. *Poor devil!* Manning thought and found his own sympathy queer, all things considered.

Ahead loomed the canyon wall and the trail's beginning. Behind them the yard was an anarchy of sound, with men calling out and men running and a gun's deep roar in the night. Manning hipped around for a look back, and he saw Torgin standing in the doorway of the house. Torgin had taken time to pull on his pants. Red blossomed where Torgin stood, and Manning knew it was Torgin doing the shooting. Gal's horse flinched as though it had been bee-stung, arched its back, and Purdy went spilling.

At once the horse was galloping off laterally, but Manning didn't waste time going after it. Purdy was down on his hands and knees, but he pulled himself to a stand. No bones broken, apparently. Manning shouted, "Here!" and leaned forward, extending a hand to Purdy, at the same time kicking his left boot free of the stirrup.

Purdy came up behind him and settled himself and wrapped his arms around Manning. "Cain't keep a good man down," Purdy roared. "Hee, hee, hee!"

Manning used his spurs. That gun was still beating behind, and once he thought he felt lead tug at his sleeve. You couldn't be sure of anything at a time like this. Your blood pounded, and excitement made you feather-light and wild-witted, and you could only keep your mind fastened to one notion: *Reach that canyon trail.*

Now they were out of six-shooter range and upon the pitch and toiling upward. Sometimes the slant was very steep, and Manning knew what had to be done. He got down from the horse and began leading it, almost running, dragging hard at the reins. Purdy made a motion to dismount. "Stay up there!" Manning shouted. He didn't want Purdy stumbling along and probably falling down every other step he took.

They were getting higher. Manning could look down on the moonlit roof of the ranch house and the yard beyond. Light fell from the open bunkhouse door; men scurried about. Over by the corrals there seemed to be massed movement, and he judged that most of the crew was saddling up. He stopped his steady climbing; he was panting, and his chest hurt. He dragged the Winchester from its scabbard and laid a few shots down there, not aiming at anything special but just kicking up the dust and giving Slash 7 something to think about. The crew scattered. Guns lighted the darkness below like malignant fireflies. Six-shooters, and the range was too great. Manning restored the Winchester and started on up the trail.

He felt like laughing, but his laughter had an edge of hysteria to it, so he quit. He sounded as bad as old Packrat. He looked down below. They'd be coming. Oh, yes, they'd be coming. He humped on upward; he'd lost count of the switchbacks. He was surprised when he saw the level of the rim before him, and soon he reached that clump of trees where he'd parted with Laura in the late afternoon.

Something stirred, and Laura emerged, astride her wagon horse. She nudged her mount forward, crying, "Cole!"

"I've gut Purdy," he said and lifted himself to the saddle. "But we've kicked up a hornet's nest. They'll be hard after us."

Laura. looked south, toward Mannington. "That way?"

Manning shook his head. "I think not. They'll expect us to head for town. What chance will we have? One horse double-loaded and you riding that work plug. Better turn north, I say. We'll have wild country to lose them in and walls ahead if we have to make a stand."

"But they may remember that dugout, too," Laura protested. "Gal found Pack-rat there."

"He found him by the creek. Remember? According to the sign, Gal didn't drop into the coulee where the dugout is. I don't think we'll have to worry about Gal, anyway. He's in no shape to ride."

From the canyon rose the rataplan of hoofs, a far furor in the night, yet near enough, near enough.

Laura's face was thoughtful in the moonlight, some excitement showing on her and perhaps a little fear.

"You're right," she cried. "And we're wasting time." She wheeled her horse to the north and belted the animal hard; and Manning swung alongside, raising his sorrel to a gallop. He felt the slap of the breeze against his face.

Chapter Thirteen

RIDERS NORTH

A few hours in bed made a difference to a man, Slade Ruxton reflected, even when the bed was as lumpy as the one in the Mannington hotel and there was only a cracked green shade to put against the afternoon's sunlight. Come to think about it, he'd slept in railroad depots and in mud wagons and on the flat tops of freight cars in his day. Slept in a tree once, for that matter. He'd learned long ago how to snatch a bit of rest whenever the chance provided. Well, there'd be better days. Once he had that twenty-five thousand dollars in his pocket, he'd have a look at San Francisco and buy himself the best bed that the best hotel provided. That was a promise, and he always kept the promises he made to himself.

San Francisco. Now there was a city that knew how to pander to a man's pleasures. Maybe the Barbary Coast wasn't what it used to be, but he was a man cut out for Nob Hill anyway, and he'd fit into the fancy life. He could drown the bleak years in champagne and forever forget them; he could take his dollars and cultivate them into more dollars. San Francisco would be only the beginning of a long golden road. Took money to make money, and with a good bag of seed in his fist, he'd know where to sow and how to reap.

Good dreaming, this, tuned to the steady clip-clop of a horse's hoofs. Around Ruxton the moonlit night stood ghostly and far reaching as he pressed northward into the Bootjack, not pushing the horse hard. He should be hurrying, he supposed, but in him was a certain reluctance to face present realities. He was on his way to Slash 7 to drive a bargain with Mack Torgin. And if he'd guessed Torgin's nature right from the pieces he'd put together about the man, Torgin would make a sharp dicker. Which meant that the twenty-five thousand dollars wouldn't be twenty-five thousand at all, but something less.

Too bad there had to be other fingers in the pie. Too bad indeed. Yet sitting in the Mannington restaurant, he'd known that he must deal with Torgin, his scheme regarding Burke Griffin having failed. Nothing had changed since. Just the same, it was vinegar in his mouth to contemplate parting with some of that Wells Fargo reward.

His long, saturnine face drew into a scowl, and his hand tightened hard on the reins. He gave a vicious tug that brought the horse's head up. He'd been a sure man across all the years, but of late some of his surety had taken a hard shaking. Too many bubbles had burst in his face. Far too many! Maybe he'd been a mite too cautious in the past; maybe the time had come to kick caution aside. One bold stroke, perhaps, and the game was won.

It was long past midnight. He should have arranged with the desk clerk to be awakened, but he hadn't supposed he'd sleep so long. Still, he'd got no sleep the night before, so nature had taken its course. Slash 7 would likely be wrapped in slumber, and it would be an odd hour for a man to pay a call, though he judged that Torgin would forgive him when the talk turned to money. But suppose he could walk into Slash 7's ranch house and out again with Purdy. That thought excited him. No need then to make a dicker and split the reward. He thought about this in the moonlight and grew bold with thinking, and desperate. Well, he could look over the situation when he got to Slash 7 and make his real decision then.

And so he rode on through the night, letting the horse set its own pace and pick its own way, so long as they skirted the west wall of the basin. When Ruxton sensed he'd come far enough, he began watching for that clump of trees that marked the canyon trail. Looked like the trees up there ahead, and at the same time he made out movement in the yonder night.

The moon was near to setting, and he strained his eyes. Then he drew to a halt and stood in his stirrups, listening. The hard pound of hoofs came to him, and the excited shouts of men, and now he made out a group of horsemen near the trees. At once his curiosity was aroused, for he'd found no other riders abroad in these small hours. They were milling about, but even as he watched, they bunched and headed south, headed straight toward him. He couldn't have fled if such had been his decision. They were on him almost at once; they surrounded him.

"Who the hell is it?" a deep voice

demanded, and Ruxton recognized the blocky figure of Mack Torgin, who found his own answer. "That stranger who's been hanging around town."

"The nosy one," someone said. "The one who's been asking questions. Looks like a gambler from the cut of his clothes. Drifted down from Butte, I'll bet. Got a marked deck in his pocket and a sneak gun up his sleeve."

Ruxton thumbed back his wide-brimmed sombrero. "My name is Slade Ruxton," he said and showed them a bold and composed face. Nearly a dozen of them by the quick count he was able to make, and no sign of that icy-eyed one he'd seen from the trees yesterday morning. Ruxton looked first for that one. Excitement had a hard hold on all of them; anger shone in their eyes and stood out in the set of their shoulders. Against the heat of their anger he must put coolness.

"I'm Torgin of Slash 7," Torgin said. "You meet anyone heading south, Ruxton? A couple fellers riding one horse, say. Maybe a girl along with them; maybe not."

Ruxton crooked one leg around his saddle horn and donned the air of an affable stranger willing to be of any possible service. "I take it you're looking for Cole Manning, Packrat Purdy, and Laura Brownlee."

Torgin jerked as though dangled from the end of a string, and suspicion deepened his voice. "Now how the hell would you know that, mister?"

"A lawman!" someone ejaculated, and moonlight glinted on a drawn gun.

Ruxton said quietly, "Put that gun away." He waited till the gun sagged in the fellow's hand, and then he smiled at Torgin. "You've called the wrong turn, friend. You can head back. There's been nobody on the trail to town."

Torgin's jaw bunched; his eyes were both skeptical and angry. "All that tangled country up north!" he said and fell to cursing.

Ruxton threw out his ace. "But I know where they've gone." He let it lie.

Torgin thrust his face close. "For a stranger, you know a helluva lot. What's your stake in this?"

"Dollars. What's yours?"

Torgin scowled. "The same thing, in the long run."

"Then maybe we could strike a deal."

Torgin's lips stayed tight. "I don't

213

know you from Adam's off ox."

"Then I'll put it plain," Ruxton said. "There's a reward for that old holdup man. Purdy can name him. I can lead you to Purdy, I think, but I'll need backing to take him away from Manning. Would you be interested in half of, say, five thousand dollars?"

"Who's putting up the reward?"

Ruxton hesitated. "Wells Fargo," he said.

"Is that old reward still standing? Mister, it used to be a lot more than five thousand dollars."

"But you've got your own stake. Doc Brownlee at your mercy, I believe."

Torgin said, "So you know about that, too."

Ruxton gave him a sardonic smile. "What I know is safe with me. All I want is what I can ride out of here with."

Torgin's eyes measured him speculatively, and then Torgin shrugged. Leather squealed faintly as Torgin shifted his weight in the saddle. "Lead the way," he said. "I won't be hoggish about the reward. You'll get what you're after, and I'll get what I want. Fair enough?"

Ruxton said, "I don't think I want to

stand up against a federal marshal."

"You won't have to," Torgin said. "Take us to him, and we'll do the rest. I'm already out on *that* limb."

Ruxton said slowly, "I've got to trust you."

Torgin said, "I'm taking the same chance on you. I've only got your word for it that Purdy isn't loping for Mannington right now. Do we string along together?"

Ruxton's mind worked rapidly. This was a better dicker than the one he might have made if Burke Griffin had shown a taste for opportunity. The deck had been reshuffled again, and now, more than ever, he needed an ally, such an ally as Mack Torgin would make. "Come along," he said and dropped his foot to the stirrup and nudged his horse northward, toward that distant coulee where an abandoned dugout stood. Mack Torgin moved up alongside him and they rode stirrup to stirrup with Slash 7's crew strung out behind.

Strong in Slade Ruxton rose the feeling that at long last he was done with caution. But Torgin had said there'd be no need for him, Ruxton, to face Cole Manning. Maybe a man could yet ride out of this without having the law hard on his heels. He hadn't burned all his bridges behind him. There was that last one left to safety.

Dr. Luke Brownlee, too, rode northward, but in the early dawn, when the dew stood on the grass and the meadow larks made bright morning music. This, Brownlee remembered, was the season between snow and summer, though he had to recollect the calendar to be sure. Got so he couldn't tell one day from another or separate the seasons, by jingo, considering how busy the hospital kept him. Man shouldn't wrap himself up so tight in his work that he wandered around in a fog, but babies did get born and people did die and sickness took no holiday.

Nice to be aboard a horse again, though he'd been so long out of saddle that tomorrow he'd likely be stiffer than a plaster cast and a fit candidate for one of his own hospital beds. Man should mind his middle so he didn't get so he overlapped a saddle horn.

Now that made something to mull over. Thirty years ago he'd been slim, a fancy figure on a horse, but he'd used a square-top buggy then and promised himself some Sunday canters he never got. Kept a saddler, too, and it got fat and lazy in its stall, while the mare that hauled the buggy did all the work. A long time dead, old Nellie, and Star, too, for that matter, though that oat-burning saddler hadn't died from overwork. Not by a long shot. Nellie had dropped in her harness, and he remembered that he'd bawled like a baby the night it happened. Many a man and woman now full grown had got safely into the world because Nellie was a sure one on the night trails and could haul a buggy from hell to breakfast. People were always thanking him for some service out of the long ago that he'd since forgotten. But who'd ever thought to thank Nellie?

Getting old, he guessed. Getting old and dwelling on the past, when it was the future he should be thinking about — the immediate future.

Done a lot of twisting and turning in bed last night. Done a lot of staring at the ceiling. Kept hearing both Ma Hibbard and Burke Griffin babbling at him, the two of them sure that Packrat Purdy was at Torgin's; they'd both been all worked up about it. Sort of put him to the test, it did. He'd snipped off a heap of arms and legs in his day, doing his operating on kitchen tables and gagging on the gas that came from chloroform vapor's being exposed to the flame of kerosene lamps; and he could remember the kind of courage it took to fight a typhoid epidemic, but he hadn't been any brave one in bed last night.

Sit tight, he'd kept telling himself. *Let things work out whichever way they're destined.* But he reckoned his worry had gone a lot deeper than Ma's or Burke Griffin's, though he wondered if they maybe knew more than they let on. Hadn't said much, only that some stranger named Ruxton had claimed that Purdy was a prisoner. Hadn't said why they thought Purdy was at Torgin's or why that had got them all lathered. But his duty had shaped up mighty plain. If he didn't head out to Slash 7, Griffin was likely to, rheumatism and all. If Purdy had anything to say, it wouldn't do for Burke to be the one to hear it.

But that was the second consideration and not the real one that got him up for an early breakfast, you bet. If anybody was going to yank Packrat Purdy out of the blaze, it was going to be yours truly, Dr. Luke Brownlee.

Then, too, there was Laura to think about — Laura skallyhooting around the basin somewhere and him closing his mind to her antics because he didn't want to think too hard about what had got Laura stirred up. But he surely had a grandfather's duty to think about, what with young Luke and his Clara both dead nearly twenty years. It had been a black day when that stagecoach had overturned crossing the flooded river with Luke and Clara trapped in it. Lucky they hadn't taken the baby along that trip. He'd known his duty toward Laura at that time, but the hospital had kept him so busy that he never even shucked out of his winter underwear till somebody came along and told him it was spring.

God, the way he'd worked over Luke and Clara the day they'd fetched him fast to that far river bank. And they both might have lived if he could have got them to the new hospital. Not enough time for that. He'd wanted that hospital so long, knowing how many Bootjack sick ones would stand a better chance with all that new, shiny equipment so close at hand; but the hospital hadn't been handy enough to save young Luke and Clara. Not by the length of eternity. It all came back to him in a black tide of memory. Well, no man was without sin, and maybe that was part of his punishment. He'd been a humbler man ever since, and a harder working one.

Troubles in the past, and troubles ahead. Mustn't let his mind dwell too much on one kind or the other. Time enough to plan what he'd do a little later. Slash 7 was still somewhere yonder. Might as well make a holiday out of the few miles between him and the ranch.

He liked this time of year and had missed too many seasons by sticking close to the hospital. New life stirring everywhere. The hills pale green and the trees showing leaf and the sage and spruce sharp-scented. Yonder a robin hauled at a worm and turned a bright, questioning eye toward horse and rider. Another month and the summer flowers would be blanketing the basin — geraniums and forget-me-nots and wild roses and sand lilies and a host of others. Just now he'd seen a few ragged dogtooth violets still holding to the shade of the pines. Made a man glad to be alive and not of a mind to dwell on trouble.

And him with his black case jostling at the saddle horn. Now why had he fetched his kit on such a mission as this? Pure habit, he guessed. Tended to the sick so long the black case had become as much a part of him as his arm. Hadn't got rich at it, but the hospital was debt-free and breaking even. Took turnips sometimes instead of cash. Took whatever they gave him and warmed his hands at gratitude's fire.

Ahead was the beginning of the canyon trail. Didn't seem possible, but there it was and no mistake about it. Daydreaming, that's what he'd been doing, he who knew every rock and tree in the Bootjack from the old days when he'd ridden far and wide to attend the sick. Easy here on the pitch, old hoss; you've got a fat man in the saddle, and he'll fall hard and his old bones are brittle. Not so fat, though, as Burke Griffin. What a sight of years he'd known Burke!

Nothing much stirring down below,

not even a wisp of smoke showing from the ranch house, and the corrals nigh empty save for some calves. Sick calves. Well, he had that against Torgin, and maybe Torgin wouldn't be too truculent, considering. Not that he'd make any bargain with Torgin that would weigh on his conscience afterward. No, siree. A messy place, Slash 7. Too bad Torgin couldn't keep his yard clean; he wasted enough time lazing around the Mannington saloons, and as likely as not his crew roundsided while the ranch grew messier. Mighty sharp turns to these switchbacks. Now where was Slash 7's crew? Gone out to work already? Couldn't be too far past regular breakfast time. One fellow there, sitting before the cookshack with his head in his hands. Lean-looking. Didn't recollect that one.

"Howdy," Brownlee said as he rode up.

The man lifted his face from his hands. Blue eyes — icy blue — the coldest eyes Brownlee had ever seen. A pair of pointed eyebrows, Mephisto-phelean eyebrows. The man said, "And who the hell are you?"

"Doc Brownlee, from Mannington."

Icy-Eyes showed him a twisted smile as though there was a big joke to be shared. "She's gone, Doc, and Manning's gone with her, and they've taken Purdy. You're a few hours too late; you missed the fireworks."

Fear stirred in Brownlee's belly like a great snake. "And Torgin's taken the crew after them?"

Icy-Eyes lifted his glance toward the empty corrals. "Judge for yourself. That's what I've had to do. I slept through the main show."

"From that bump on your temple? Let me have look at it."

"I didn't send for you, Doc."

"Never mind." Brownlee got down from the saddle and unfastened the black case and opened it. "No stitches needed," he said, making his inspection. "I'll swab you off and put a pad on that goose egg. Head's throbbing like a war drum, I'll bet." He dug into the black case till he found what he wanted. "Here, swallow this sedative. It will ease you."

A plague on the hold habit got on a man! Here was Laura gone and Packrat gone and Manning with them — that would be Flint's boy that the papers had been shouting about — and Torgin hot on their trail. A devil's broth all stirred up for sure. High time to be riding — riding hard; but here was work for the hand, and a doctor was a doctor always. Look back across all the years and it had been that way, somebody else's need coming first; but he guessed he was too old a dog to learn any new tricks. And maybe that was part of the paying for old sins; maybe Luke's and Clara's passing hadn't been enough.

A cool one, this icy-eyed patient, not flinching when the iodine bit, taking that capsule down like it was a chunk of candy. There! It was done, and a fairly fancy job for a fast one. "Go stretch out on one of the bunks," Brownlee said. "That medicine will make you sleep around the clock. When you wake up, you'll never know you were hurt."

Those blue eyes blazed at him. "I've got riding to do! Damn it, you drugged me, Doc!"

"You'll be better off for it. Which way did Torgin head?"

"If I knew, I wouldn't tell you. I didn't ask you to open your blasted kit, re-member!"

"Better get into a bunk, son."

Brownlee climbed up into the saddle again and took to the canyon trail. Easy, old hoss, easy till we get to the top. You can stretch your legs then.

No need to puzzle about Torgin; since Slash 7 hadn't turned south, they must have gone north. To that old dugout on the abandoned homestead. Sure as shooting! That was where Laura had been hiding out Packrat Purdy, for Ma Hibbard had told Brownlee so. He reached under his coat and hauled out a Colt forty-five and had a look at the loads. Long time since he'd packed a gun — a mighty long time. He'd thought twice about taking it today. Felt heavy, uncommonly heavy. A strange instrument to the hand of a healing man.

Chapter Fourteen

THE END OF VALOR

In the darkness of the coulee dugout, the thick darkness before dawn, Cole Manning heard Laura grope toward him and felt the gentle pressure of her fingers on his arm. "Everything's done that can be done," she said. "Why don't you snatch some sleep, Cole? You couldn't have got much rest in that root cellar."

"How about you?" he asked.

"We'll take turn about. You first, though. You're the one who'll need to be fresh if Slash 7 trails us here. Packrat and I will keep each other company and stand watch besides. Now go lie down on the bunk."

"Guess you're right," Manning said. He felt drawn tighter than a fiddle string. He found his way to the bunk and stretched himself out, not even bothering to remove his boots. Laura came to him and tugged at his boots. He didn't try to stop her; he was too tired for that. He murmured a drowsy thanks.

Packrat Purdy was a quiet one in a

far corner. "Got it figgered out now," he said. "You ain't Flint. You're Flint's boy growed up."

"That's right," Manning said sleepily. There was a whole passel of questions he wanted to ask Purdy, and maybe there was no better time than now. Trouble was, he was too tired for talking, and his mind kept shuttling every which direction. He guessed everything had been done that could be done, just as Laura had said. They'd come here through the night far enough ahead of any pursuit so that they hadn't felt pushed, yet they'd quirted hard. That hobbled work horse Laura had left near the wagon had been gone; but when they'd cut sign, they'd seen that the animal had made its way into that other coulee to the creek. After some discussion, they'd turned Laura's own unsaddled mount into that same coulee and fetched Manning's double-burdened sorrel to the makeshift barn out yonder.

Manning hadn't unsaddled, merely loosening the cinch. No telling how fast they might have to get out of here, and he'd wondered if the other horses shouldn't be kept handy, too.

"I'm hungry," Packrat had said.

They'd made him be content with a cold meat sandwich. No smoke must show, and no light. Manning had fetched the guns into the dugout, his forty-five and his Winchester. He had a few rounds for the Colt in his belt and a spare box of rifle shells which he'd toted in his saddlebag. Laura contributed a few revolver shells she'd been carrying in her pocket for the gun she'd lost in her cutbank encounter with Manning.

Manning had frowned at this sorry collection. Two guns, and two men to handle them, but not much ammunition if a siege shaped up. Still, these log walls were stout; and with the dugout backed up against the coulee's slope, no one could get at them from behind. They'd spend the day here, he decided; and if all stayed quiet, they'd try for Mannington under cover of darkness.

So thinking, he dozed and then slept soundly, though it seemed he'd no more than got himself comfortable when Laura shook him gently.

"They're here," she said, her voice so calm that he didn't at first understand.

He looked about him and saw that the gray of morning was in the dugout. He swung his legs to the earth floor, got into his boots, and crept with Laura to the one window. He could see the openness between the dugout and the first bushes, and in the clearing a huddled group of horsemen sat their saddles, studying the place. They'd just arrived, Manning judged. Torgin bulked big among them.

"Think they'll go away without looking inside?" Laura whispered.

"Not a chance," Manning said. "They're just getting set to Injun up. Hand me the rifle."

He laid the Winchester across the sill, sighted carefully, and squeezed the trigger. Dust erupted at the feet of Torgin's horse, and the mount reared. Torgin's deep voice lifted to a startled roar; he flailed wildly with his free hand. Slash 7 wheeled about and galloped down the coulee. Manning sent a shot after them.

"They'll be back," he prophesied. "On foot."

Now how in blazes had they come so unerringly to this coulee? Not by tracking across the rocky terrain that had baffled Manning his first day in the Bootjack and made Torgin give up his pursuit of Laura's wagon. Gal? But even if Gal had proved to be up to riding, he could only have brought them to this general vicinity.

"Anybody in town know you were using this place for a hide-out?" Manning asked Laura.

"Only Ma Hibbard," she replied. "And you can bet she wouldn't have told. Besides, Torgin hasn't had time to get to Mannington and back again."

Manning thought of Slade Ruxton then. Ruxton had been to this very dugout. Had the careful one grown desperate and therefore careless? He shook his head. He hadn't seen Ruxton out there with Slash 7, but he couldn't be sure, not with the light so uncertain. His knees ached from crouching by this window. He looked at Laura; her face was composed, her cheeks showing only a faint flush of excitement. She'd do to side a man in a tight; she'd long since proved that.

He glanced through the window. "Someone moving out there," he reported, and bullets rattled against the log wall, an angry fusillade.

"Get back!" he shouted at Laura. "They're on foot and hunkering in the bushes."

Packrat Purdy came close to Manning. "Gimme a gun!" the old eccentric shouted and lifted Manning's forty-five from its holster. He fired three times in rapid succession through the window; Manning saw leaves clipped from the bushes.

"None of that," Manning cried and batted at Purdy's arm. "We haven't got the powder to burn."

He knew now what they must do. Somehow this ruse of coming to the coulee had gone wrong, and so they were in for a siege. No two ways about that. They could keep Torgin's crew from rushing the dugout as long as they had lead to throw at Slash 7. But no sense in wasting it. Let Torgin's bunch chip bark from the log wall and batter bullets against the closed door. The window was the only vulnerable spot.

A bullet sang through the window and brought the rusty stovepipes down with a clatter. Manning risked peering out. He saw one man, bolder than the rest, edging out from cover, crouched low, and stepping forward. Manning took the forty-five from Purdy and snapped a quick shot. Getting light enough for good shooting now. The Slash 7 man

231

howled, dropped his gun, and clutched at his left forearm and beat fast for shelter.

Thus it was to go through the weary morning, with Slash 7 playing safe by lying hidden and venting its anger in an occasional volley and once in a while some one growing bold and being sorry for it. Manning had to maintain constant vigilance, and his neck ached from strain. A few times he'd come close to being clipped when he showed himself to send back a shot.

Near noon Torgin raised a shout. "All we want is Purdy. Send him out, and we'll call off this show."

Manning answered him with a bullet and at once regretted the waste. There weren't too many shells left.

"We gonna eat?" Purdy demanded.

Manning said over his shoulder, "Might as well fix some food, Laura. Careful, now! Just be sure you keep out of line with the window."

She didn't try building a fire, not with the stovepipes knocked down. No use smoking themselves out of their own stronghold. Manning ate the cold meat and bread she handed him, crouched beside the window, and was glad for those supplies she'd brought from town.

"Hope they're getting good and hungry," he said.

"They can always send a man back to Slash 7 for grub," Laura observed.

But Manning judged that there was no diminution in the strength of the besiegers and grew more convinced of this as the afternoon dragged on. The hours had become an endlessness of discouraging the bold ones and standing ready against anyone's venturesomeness. He took to using the Winchester again, for he wished to conserve such few forty-five shells as were left. He'd need them for close-up work when darkness came and Torgin could make a rush.

That was the rub. The present advantage of the besieged was daylight, these droning sunlit hours. But what would happen when night fell? This thought nagged constantly at Manning, filling him with foolhardy notions.

Try rushing across the openness and thus gain the other coulee? They'd cut him down before he'd taken three steps. Try to reach the barn and his horse in the hopes of then skirting the besiegers and running for Mannington and help? That would be even riskier than the first notion. Maybe he could make a dicker with Torgin. But Torgin had already stated his terms and had them refused. No, there was nothing to do but play out this hand in the present manner.

He'd used up the last of the Winchester shells when evening came, so he discarded the empty rifle. Its only usefulness would be as a club to help stave off a rush. He spaced out his forty-five shells as the twilight deepened into night. Not enough shells — not nearly enough. Packrat huddled in a corner, made weary and fretful by the endless day. Laura's face showed the strain of the hours.

Manning forced a grin as he looked at them in the gathering gloom. "Nothing much left but the victory celebration," he said.

Laura said, "I think they're up to something. I'm sure that only about half of them have been shooting this last twenty minutes or so."

Purdy stared upward. "Maybe they're Injuning around to get onto the roof."

Manning shook his head. "It's dirt, and too thick to let a bullet through. If they started clawing a hole, we could make it hot for them from this side."

"Look!" Laura cried. "They've got my wagon and are pushing it up the coulee."

Manning risked a look and drew a bullet which made him jerk back his head. But he'd seen that Laura was right; three or four of Slash 7's crew had reversed the wagon and were pushing it forward by its tongue, keeping the wagon box between themselves and the dugout.

"A fire wagon," Manning said, getting the idea, and hope died in him.

Torgin's voice rose. "We've got it loaded with dry brush. We can push it right against your door and set it ablaze. You're down to your forty-five, Manning, and I know it. Toss it out here or take a toasting."

"Here it is," Manning said and flung the gun through the window.

"The rifle, too," Torgin shouted. "Just to play safe." Manning picked up the Winchester and sent it after the Colt.

This, then, was the end of valor, for it had to be, he reflected. Funny how Flint Manning crept into your thoughts in the tight moments and you fell to wondering what he'd have done in a moment like this. Not that it mattered. This was today and now, and you could go on being brave till you died from bravery and with you Laura and an old man who wasn't quite right in the head and therefore was your responsibility. The coulee dugout had seemed a good gamble in the darkness before dawn, but it had made a sorry ace, and the game was finished.

Torgin's men shaped up in the gathering dusk, coming forward cautiously. No guns now to stop them. They grew bolder with each step; they swarmed forward and the door of the dugout flew open and Torgin was here, his gun sweeping in a wide arc to cover the interior. A couple of his men crowded in after him. Torgin let out a gusty sigh, and his eyes were hot as he looked at Manning. "You gave us a bad day, mister."

"You've got worse ones coming," Manning said. "I'm still wearing a badge, remember."

Torgin put a shoulder to the wall and showed a wicked smile. "Time's past for worrying about that. I crawled out on the limb the minute I heaved you into the root cellar last night. But maybe you'll overlook my shortcomings. Ever wonder why the great Flint Manning failed on that old case, kid? Do you reckon Flint didn't *want* to find the man who did that robbery?" He spoke to his men. "Get a light going, will you?"

Someone found the lantern and lighted it and placed it upon the table.

Torgin looked at Packrat. "Now we'll get it over with," Torgin said.

Purdy backed up against the wall, his eyes frantic. "I don't know nuthin'!"

Torgin took a step toward Purdy and slapped Purdy across the mouth with the back of his free hand. "You know where you got that jewelry!" Torgin thundered. "You stole it from someone, and that someone must have been the holdup man. Who was it! Speak up!"

Laura took an angry step forward, but a Slash 7 man pushed at her, shoving her back. She staggered, almost losing her balance. Three of Torgin's men were in the dugout now; the rest seemed to be clustered outside. Laura's voice lashed at Torgin. "Why are you so interested in that old case? Are you afraid of what Packrat may know? You were here in the old days. Maybe you're the man who robbed that stagecoach!"

Torgin laughed. "I think you know better than that, girl. In any case, you're talking about a deal that happened three or four years before you were born. If you're curious, you should talk to some of the old-timers. You'd find out that I happen to be the one man in Bootjack Basin who couldn't possibly have been the phantom. *I* was riding the stage the night it was robbed — a passenger. And I had a good look at the holdup man. He was masked, but for years I've had a sneaking hunch who he was. Now I'll get the proof."

He glared at Purdy. "Come on, speak up!" he demanded. "Who had that jewelry before you toted it off?"

"I ain't saying," Purdy insisted.

Torgin ran his tongue along his lips, his broad face lupine in the lantern light. "One of you boys stir up a fire in that junk heap of a stove," he ordered. "And go scrounge around the place for something that will pass for a running iron. We'll unlock this jigger's jaw."

Wild fear leaped into Purdy's eyes, but a valiant stubbornness was there, too. "I won't talk," he said. "You can't make me talk."

Manning, tense and silent, was suddenly sure that Purdy wouldn't talk, either. And Torgin was doubtful, too, from the look of him. His eyes hotter with anger, he studied Purdy for a long moment, then glanced at Laura. "Get that iron," he ordered again. "We'll still use it. Only we'll use it on the girl. Maybe that will open up Purdy."

One of his men said uneasily, "Hell, Mack, we can't go that far!"

Torgin said, "We've gone so far already there's no choice. Do you think I'm stopping when I'm this near getting what I want? Start a fire, I say!"

Manning lunged toward Torgin; but a gun, digging into Manning's ribs, stopped him. The gun was in the hands of one of Torgin's men, and Torgin swung his own weapon in Manning's direction. "Don't try that again," Torgin said.

Purdy crouched low, and Manning was sure the addled old fellow was going to leap at Torgin and be stopped by a bullet and that would be the end of it. One of Torgin's men moved toward the stove and lifted a lid. He was the one who'd sat before Slash 7's cookshack last night with his hat slanted low and his jaw hard. His jaw was as hard now; he was not balking at torture as Gal had balked. Manning had never expected to find himself hoping for the appearance of Gal, but he hoped for it now.

Then all the stubbornness ran out of Purdy, and his shoulders slumped. "I'll talk," he said hoarsely. "You leave Laura alone, and I'll talk."

"Then do it," Torgin snapped.

"It was a long time ago it happened," Purdy blurted. "It was the same night the stage was held up, only I didn't know about that. I was out a-lookin' at the moon, and I saw a man come riding with a big ironbound box balanced on his saddle horn. One of them green Wells Fargo boxes. He got off his horse and buried the box. When he was gone, I dug it up. It had all them pretty jewels in it, so I took 'em home. Hid 'em under the floor of my shack and nobody ever found 'em. Had 'em up to play with the day Burke Griffin come looking for that saddle. He took 'em away and put me in jail."

Torgin leaned forward. "The holdup man hid the jewels because they were too dangerous to handle. Just as I guessed. But who was he, Purdy?"

The oldster ran his eyes from one face to another, and it was a moment when the sound of a man's breathing was like the gusty rush of wind in a high mountain pass. Purdy's eyes locked with Manning's; Purdy's eyes begged forgiveness. He pointed a finger at Manning. "Him."

"You're crazy!" Torgin shouted.

But Manning understood and was sick with the knowledge, remembering the mistake Purdy had made earlier, remembering Purdy's saying at Slash 7, "But don't you worry. I didn't tell 'em a thing — "

Purdy now shook his head in bewilderment. "No, not him. He's Flint's kid. But I've told you, and you've got to leave Laura alone like you promised. The feller that buried the box was Flint Manning."

Chapter Fifteen

DEEP NIGHT

This was a moment that held for Manning the taint of nightmare, yet the reality was sharp enough. Flint Manning, lawman and legend, a stage robber? Flint Manning, peace officer by day, phantom rider by night? Cole Manning shook his head. Yet once, thinking of Burke Griffin, he'd remembered that the Bootjack stood next door to vigilante country, and a man had only to turn back the pages of Montana's history to find a sheriff who'd secretly been a king-pin outlaw. And perhaps Torgin had hinted at the same thing when he'd asked, "Do you reckon Flint didn't *want* to find the man who did that robbery?"

You could twist and squirm in your mind, seeking a loophole in your own mad thinking; but all the while you'd been warned, if only you'd had an ear for listening. What was it Laura had said? "You'll keep hunting and hunting, I know. Till you come to the end of the trail. And then it will be too late for you to see that you should never have started."

This, then, was the end of the trail.

But Mack Torgin was finding no triumph in the moment. His face wicked with anger, Torgin slapped Purdy again. "You're lying!" Torgin said hoarsely. "You're lying, confound you! Trying to play safe by pinning the robbery on a dead man!"

Purdy cringed against the wall, his hair tousled, his eyes frantic. "I ain't lying. I didn't want to speak up. Flint, he was real good to me when he was sheriff. He never put me in jail when I took things, he didn't."

"I was on that stagecoach," Torgin stormed. "And I saw the man who held it up. I've told you that. I kept my eyes and ears open afterward. Shortly, a certain gent in Mannington began spreading money around. He claimed he'd inherited it from some relative back East. I couldn't brand him a liar. But I've watched and waited all these years, figuring that some day I'd find the proof. It wasn't Flint Manning who buried that loot, Purdy, and you know it. It was Doc Brownlee!"

Laura's laugh was scornful. "So you

hope to put Gramp at your mercy and force through your packing-plant scheme!"

It fits, Manning thought. *It makes sense out of Torgin's threat to Doc Brownlee in the hospital.* "The whole damn town will side you, Doc," Torgin had said. "But one of these days I may have something to hand them that even Griffin will have to heed."

"It was Flint Manning," Purdy insisted. "How can I say it was Doc buried that box when it wasn't?"

And Cole Manning was sick with the certainty that Packrat Purdy was speaking the truth. It showed on Purdy, plain as print. Even Mack Torgin was now convinced, for disappointment drew taut his black-browed face. Silence filled the dugout, broken only by the batting against the lantern of some winged things drawn out of the night, that and the shuffling of boots of the men who clustered outside.

A closed case, Manning reflected; he'd discovered who'd robbed that stage long years ago. A need to laugh filled him.

He could choose now between his blood and his badge, for he'd either have to report a failure or report the infamy of Flint Manning. Out of chaotic thinking came an odd wonder. Would they still leave the statue standing in Mannington? And then the short hairs at the nape of his neck prickled, for suddenly he was cold with the knowledge that he wasn't going to be allowed to make any choice. He could see his doom in Mack Torgin's eyes, for Torgin was studying all three prisoners with a deep and desperate speculation.

"We're in a tight, boys," Torgin said slowly. "We're in a bad tight. If Purdy had named Doc, we could have put the whole basin over a barrel. As it is, we've mauled a marshal and made talk of torturing a girl. We can't let them carry that tale back to town. Not now."

The Slash 7 man who'd showed uneasiness earlier headed out the door. "I'm drifting," he said, but that hard-jawed one stood his ground. "This lawman was looking for Purdy, wasn't he?" he asked, nodding toward Manning. "Suppose he'd caught up with him. Suppose there'd been a shoot-out."

Torgin's eyes squinted down. "I'm not sure I follow you."

"It's pat. The Brownlee girl dresses like a boy. Manning might have put a

245

bullet into her before he guessed the truth. Don't you see? Then him and Packrat could have shot it out. Three dead ones strewed out proper, with fired guns in their hands, would tell their own story."

Torgin gave this his consideration; and strong in Manning was the remembrance of the root cellar at Slash 7 and Laura saying in the darkness, "The more desperate Torgin gets, the more dangerous he'll become." Manning looked straight at Torgin and said, "Mack, you'll never get away with this. Don't be a damned fool, Mack!"

But Torgin didn't seem to hear him. Torgin's eyes had turned bolder. "Yes, it's pat," he said. "A pat hand."

"You promised not to hurt Laura!" Purdy shrilled. He flailed his hands, his voice rising to a steady shriek. "Help! Help! Help!"

"Quit that!" Manning said sternly. "You're wasting your breath."

Then he lunged at the man nearest him, that hard-jawed one. Nothing left now but the desperate need to make some kind of play and go down fighting. He struck out blindly, his fist thudding against the fellow, but it was a short blow with no heft behind it. Too crowded here to get in a good swing. But amazingly, the man went down, blood gushing from his shoulder. No fist had done that damage, Manning realized dazedly. A gun had boomed out in the gathering darkness.

Someone had fired through the open doorway, and the bullet spread consternation. Torgin made a wild dive toward the door. "Outside!" he boomed. "Get outside and scatter! Douse that light, somebody!"

Panic had caught those clustered beyond the door, and they were stampeding. That distant gun spoke again. "Must be Burke Griffin," someone shouted. "Maybe he's got a posse!" Manning was sure he recognized Slade Ruxton's voice.

Torgin and the two other Slash 7 men in the dugout were jammed in the doorway, their voices frantic. The long day had drawn them fine, and fear had finally snapped them. They got outside; their boots pounded in retreat. They were running for the shelter of the bushes, firing as they went. And somewhere in the darkness that other gun beat steadily. Whoever was firing was a friend, no doubt of that, but he was alone, Manning judged, a fact which Torgin's bunch would be quick to discover once their first panic passed.

Manning took abrupt advantage of the confusion. Blowing out the lantern, he got hold of the wrists of Laura and Packrat. "Come on!" he urged and dragged them from the dugout.

That lone gunman was somewhere in the bushes up the west slope of the coulee. Manning saw the flash of his gun. Timber topped the ridge; Manning could see its serrated outline against the sky. Torgin and his men had headed down the coulee. Out in the open, Manning recognized the danger of being caught in a cross fire, but the man on the slope shouted, "This way. Laura, do you hear me?"

"Gramp!" Laura cried.

Manning let go of Purdy and scooped up the forty-five he'd thrown from the window. How many shots were left? No time now to load.

He ran toward the makeshift barn and led out his saddler and hurriedly tightened the cinch. He boosted Laura into the saddle, belted the horse across the rump with his sombrero and sent it bolting toward the slope. He ran after the horse, Purdy pounding along beside him. They clawed into the bushes and began climbing the slope. Brownlee's voice guided them. High up, they came upon Brownlee's crouched figure. Laura had found him, too.

"Keep going," Brownlee said. "My horse is above." He fumbled fresh cartridges into his gun and stood up. He laid three evenly spaced shots at the gun flames winking from the coulee's bottom.

Slash 7's firing was sporadic, and Manning wondered how many others in the crew had decided to bolt. Manning filled his own gun and held it in his hand as he toiled on upward with Purdy and Laura. Brownlee came stumbling after them. They got into the timber at the top of the ridge, and Brownlee said, "Over this way." Manning made out a tied horse.

"Climb on with me, Packrat," Brownlee said.

Purdy did as directed, and Manning swung up behind Laura. Brownlee led the way, moving south along the ridge. Boots rattled rock in the darkness; a couple of Torgin's bunch seemed to be scaling the slope. In pursuit? Manning hipped around, keening the night, his gun lifted. Torgin's men had horses and soon might be moving back to them. Or had Slash 7 got a bellyful of this whole affair?

A mile to the south, Brownlee suddenly veered due east. The ridge had petered out, and the timber had thinned. Brownlee led them down off the slope and across the basin's floor. Now they could move at a high gallop, but they soon had to pull the double-burdened horses to a walk. Brownlee's face was calm in the early starlight. "They'll be expecting us to line out straight for town," he said. "Maybe we can fool them."

Manning remembered that he'd tried a comparable ruse early this morning, only to be trapped in the coulee. But there had been Slade Ruxton to point Torgin's way — Manning was sure of that now — and Slash 7 had been more zealous then.

The silent night now crowded round. They moved through the night; they came across the basin to Bootjack River and worked south along the bank, keeping to the willows' cover. They skirted the river for nearly a mile, riding single file. Then they rested the horses again and sat listening; far away rose the rumor of men traveling. Manning said, "Sounds like only a couple. Torgin's got a scared crew. They climbed out on the limb with Torgin tonight, and the limb broke."

Laura said, "I was never so glad to see you, Gramp."

"I was there on the slope most of the day," Brownlee said. "You were under siege when I arrived. I could do no good by revealing my presence, and I was afraid to turn back to town for help, so I bided my time. I risked a shot when I heard Packrat scream. It was chancy, with that dugout packed, but it was the best I could do."

"Ma Hibbard told you where to find me?"

Brownlee nodded. "Laura, the time has come for the truth. What gave you the notion of snatching Purdy out of jail in the first place?"

"You did, Gramp," she said. "You've been worried sick ever since Purdy was arrested. You even told Ma Hibbard you hoped Packrat couldn't identify the robber. You argued it was better if old ghosts were left lying. There's a skeleton in your closet, Gramp. If I could get Purdy free before he spoke out of turn, I could bury that skeleton. But Torgin made Purdy speak up tonight. We know the truth now. It's as Ma Hibbard and I suspected all along. Flint Manning was your friend, so you didn't want his name blackened."

Cole Manning said, "You know me, don't you, Doc?"

"Of course," Brownlee said. "This is the first chance I've had for this." He extended his hand. "You've grown to be a fine-looking man. I think Flint would be proud of you."

"I wanted to wear a badge," Manning said. "Now I wish I'd never seen one. What kind of report can I turn in? It will be a big day for the headline hunters. 'Cole Manning Proves Famous Father Was Highwayman.' "

Brownlee said, "Your father didn't hold up that stage."

"Then who did?"

Brownlee's face looked old in the star-shine, yet he showed a certain serenity like a man soon to be freed of a burdensome knowledge. It was a moment before he spoke. "My statement alone won't do," he said. "It's proof that's got to be put in your hand. I'll turn that proof over to you in Mannington. Let's ride again."

The night was nearly gone when the four rode in, single-filing between the two rows of false fronts that marked the main street. They had followed a slow, circuitous trail, resting often; and no man had barred that trail, and no man showed on the street. But strong in Manning was the thought of Mack Torgin turned doubly desperate, and thus Manning's wariness was no less sharp now that the town had been attained. He was tired and mixed up in his thinking yet strangely exhilarated for all that.

They paused before a darkened cottage at one end of the street, and here Brownlee stiffly dismounted and went up a path to thunder at the cottage door.

"Burke Griffin's place," Laura explained.

A door opened, and there was talk; the door closed again. Brownlee came back, saying nothing, a ring of keys in his hand. He motioned the others to follow and walked toward the jail building. They tied the horse at the hitchrack, and Brownlee unlocked the office and got the lamp lighted. He glanced back into the cell beyond the office. No one there, Manning judged, for Brownlee shook his head.

Griffin came through the open doorway, looking sleepy, looking troubled, his trousers hastily pulled on over his nightgown, one suspender dangling. "All right, Doc," he said.

"Sorry to break your rest, Burke," Brownlee said, "but this can't keep any longer. Find that letter Flint Manning gave you years ago when you were his deputy. You know, the one to be opened if anybody ever was brought to trial for that old stage robbery."

Griffin shook his head. "You really want it, Doc?"

"I really want it."

Griffin shrugged. "Sure," he said. Taking the ring of keys from Brownlee, he unlocked a desk drawer and lifted a chamois bag from the litter within. "The Wells Fargo jewels," he said absently. He pawed at a heap of papers. "Here it is," he said and passed over a sealed letter.

Brownlee handed it to Manning. "Read it, boy," he urged. "Read it aloud for all of us."

Puzzled, Manning ran his thumb under the flap, shook out the folded pages, and recognized the handwriting of his father. The letter was dated March, 1892. Very slowly he began to read:

" 'Old ghosts have a habit of riding again. Therefore, since circumstances might some day pin a certain unsolved crime on an innocent party, it has been agreed between me and my friend Dr. Luke Brownlee that this letter should be left to come to light if ever there is a need for it.

" 'Four years ago a sack of mail and a Wells Fargo shipment of jewelry and a payroll consigned to an Idaho mining syndicate were lifted from a stagecoach by a masked, armed robber. When this holdup was reported to me by the coach's driver and passenger, I, in my capacity as sheriff, took the trail of the robber.

" 'Cutting sign on him was a simple job. The man was obviously an amateur. I overtook him in the vicinity of Packrat Purdy's shack late that very night and put him under arrest — the hardest task of my life, for he was a man beloved by all Bootjack Basin, Dr. Brownlee.

" 'When I demanded an explanation, he confessed that he had taken the money in desperation. Fighting a typhoid fever epidemic at the time, he knew the crying need of the basin for an equipped hospital. More than that, with the basin's population growing, each year would see a greater need for such a hospital. As he talked of his plans and dreams, I was convinced of his sincerity and selflessness, and thus I made a decision which I have never since regretted.

" 'On the one hand there was money belonging to a mining syndicate which could stand its loss a hundred times over — a syndicate with a reputation for double-dealing. On the other hand, there was the good that could come from Brownlee's use of that money. There were cripples who would walk, sick who would get well. I have been called a town builder, and I helped to build one that night.

" 'Doc Brownlee could keep the money as far as I was concerned. The mail, which he had taken only to make the robbery appear valid, we would forward a few letters at a time so as not to arouse suspicion. The jewelry would be returned to Wells Fargo after the excitement died down. I took the strong box with the jewelry and buried it close by. When I returned for it weeks later, the jewelry was gone. And that is the main reason for this letter. If some innocent party stumbled onto the jewelry and kept it, presuming it to be loot from an older robbery of bygone lawless days, that party might some day be accused of the robbery. Dr. Brownlee and I do not want that to happen. He is the man who robbed the stage, and I, in a sense, was his accomplice.

" 'To those who may judge us harshly, I suggest an examination of the records of Brownlee's charity hospital.' "

Manning's voice droned to a stop and faded, like ghostly hoofbeats fading back into the past. He looked about him, seeing Purdy's bewildered face and Laura's still one. Griffin, too, showed no emotion; Brownlee made a weary gesture with his hand.

"Now you see why Purdy thought Flint

257

was the robber," Brownlee said in the heavy silence. "No matter what name we gave it, it was still robbery. Burke, I suppose you'll want to lock me up till Manning can take me to Helena."

"Shucks, Doc, I ain't never had a cell your size in my jail," Griffin said. "You see, I read that letter years ago and sealed it up again. Always did have too big a bump of curiosity. When I found that jewelry in Purdy's shack, I would have kept shut, only I reckoned Flint would want it returned to Wells Fargo. Looked like I had no choice but to fetch in Purdy. Then the big-town newspapers got hold of the story and played it up. So I had to keep Packrat in jail till young Manning got here. Only Packrat got away. Now you'll understand why I went hunting you, all excited, when that Ruxton feller mentioned Packrat's being held prisoner. I knew Torgin was gunning for you, so I figgered it must be Torgin had him. Well, the cat's out of the bag now. But I'll turn in my badge before I'll turn a key on you, Doc."

Laura shook her head. "Ma Hibbard supposed it was Flint's name you were worried about, Gramp. I did what I thought you'd want me to do. I'm proud of you for facing up to the truth."

"Wait!" Manning cried. "Wait till I think — "

From the open doorway, Mack Torgin said, "I'll save you the trouble." He stood there with a gun steady in his hand. "You folks weren't hard to find, burning the only light in town. I heard every word of that letter. Pass it over, Manning. Pass it over, I say."

Slade Ruxton stood at Torgin's shoulder, his sardonic face showing its faint hint of laughter. He, too, held a gun. "Slash 7's crew has deserted," he said. "I alone stayed with the sinking ship. But I'm no such fool as to figure there'll be any gold for me in Flint Manning's noble confession. I think I'll take something more tangible. Those Wells Fargo jewels, Sheriff. Would they be in that chamois sack on your desk?"

Manning said, "I credited you with better sense, Ruxton."

Ruxton shrugged. "The safe way has proved to be too slow. Here's where I burn a last bridge behind me."

Manning moved then, turned desperate by Torgin's desperation, and Ruxton's. His left arm flailed out, pushing

Laura away; she stumbled and sat down heavily. And in that moment Manning lunged hard against the desk and sent the lamp crashing to darkness.

Chapter Sixteen

SECOND CHOICE

In the confines of this little office, the roar of a forty-five made a mighty thunder, filling the corners and beating back from the walls. Torgin shooting, Manning judged, though he couldn't be sure, not with the darkness all around. He still held Flint Manning's letter in his hand. He jammed the letter inside his shirt and got his own gun out and sent a shot in the direction of the doorway, and then he leaped straight at the doorway. He was mindful that four others besides himself were packed in here and that one of them was Laura. He had to carry the fight outside and put an end to it.

He was shouting, he realized, "Down! All of you!" That was advice for Griffin and Purdy and Brownlee, but his voice must be carrying a warning to Torgin and Ruxton. Those two now knew he was coming at them.

He could make out the doorway; the darkness beyond was filled with black shapes and black shadows in the starlight. Frantic movement yonder; and when he charged through the doorway, Torgin and Ruxton were spilling down the steps, beating a retreat. Thus the payoff to a desperate gamble. It had been Manning's hope that he could demoralize the two by showing fight.

Ruxton was ahead and running hard, Torgin close behind him, his stride the awkward one of a man whose boots were too tight for him. Manning vaulted over the hitchrail where his sorrel and Doc Brownlee's horse stood tied. Torgin turned, falling into a crouch. His gun blossomed, and Manning felt the close wind of that bullet; and the two horses began rearing and pitching, not bullet-stung but boogered.

Manning had no thought in him then; he only squeezed at the trigger. It wasn't until Torgin fell into an ungainly heap, his dream of intimidation ended, that Manning remembered the coulee dug-out and the talk of torture and so found no regret.

Ruxton was legging it down the street. Manning sprinted after him, a hot fury growing. Someone called to Manning from the porch of the jail building; he recognized the voice as Griffin's. "Stay back there!" Manning shouted. Ruxton was the dangerous one, he knew. Ruxton was already hard to find, running along the dark street and not being so foolish as to turn and shoot and thus make himself plain. The ticket was to keep him in sight.

Manning kept running. Windows were banging open here and there and sleepy voices calling. Ruxton had cut across the street toward the hospital; and when Manning reached the shadowy entrance, he paused, pulled short by caution.

Had Ruxton gone inside? He didn't think so. But the street lay dark and formless, and an unwary man could easily be ambushed anywhere along it. Manning strained his eyes; they were growing accustomed to the darkness, and it seemed to him that the dawn was close. He strained his ears, too. Birds were making their early-morning racket in the cottonwoods, but he thought he heard the merest whisper of another sound. A boot sole against the boardwalk? He couldn't be sure. He moved on down the street as silently as he could.

Now he felt a tightness to his back muscles and a squeamishness in his stomach. He clutched his gun so hard that his fingers ached. Ruxton and Torgin must have had horses somewhere. Manning supposed that Ruxton might be trying to reach his horse and so clear town. Yet he judged that the two had left their mounts near the jail building, possibly in a vacant lot. Each step was taking the hunt farther from the jail. Ruxton, then, must have fled in blind panic, but he'd had time now to recover from his panic and be a cool one playing a cool game. Where, then, would the finish of it be?

Someone was calling to Manning from the vicinity of the jail, but he didn't so much as look over his shoulder. He was nearly to the far end of the street, and Ruxton might as well have been swallowed by the earth. Silvery light now outlined the eastern hills, and ahead reared the statue of Flint Manning, faintly silhouetted. Cole Manning looked toward the statue and thought he saw movement at its base.

"Ruxton?" he called.

A soft stirring yonder — something not really seen not heard. But now he

264

knew that Ruxton was behind the base of the statue.

"Ruxton," he called again. "Toss away your gun and come out of there." An idea stirred in him that was as vague as the shadows beyond; he wanted words to get that idea across to Ruxton, but he couldn't find them. "Ruxton, I've got nothing against you that makes me want your scalp."

Ruxton said, "So you're still loaded down with ideals, you damn fool," and his gun made a redness in the dawn, the bullet thunking solidly into the side of the building by which Manning stood.

Manning fired instinctively, having only Ruxton's gun flash for target. Ruxton had exposed himself to get that one shot. He came forward now, taking three short, mincing steps before he crumpled. He went to his knees first and then toppled over slowly. Manning walked toward him and looked down at the sprawled figure and knew Ruxton to be dead.

He cased his gun and walked back as far as the planking and seated himself on the boardwalk's edge. Aftermath overcame him then; he had never killed a man before tonight, but there'd been no time to think about that when Torgin had gone down. He'd tossed lead at Slash 7 and nicked at least one man at the coulee siege, but this was different. Now he felt very ill and was certain his stomach was going to rebel. He fought against nausea. He looked up at the statue of Flint Manning and wondered if the great one had known such a moment as this and realized with certainty that Flint Manning had. In what strange town, on what far trail?

He heard his name called cautiously from a distance and recognized Laura's voice. He got up and walked toward her.

She came to him running; she came into his arms. She asked, "Are you hurt, Cole? Are you hurt?"

"No," he said and shrugged. "At least there'll be no scar that shows."

"Let's get off the street before the whole town is here asking questions," she said. She took his arm. "Come along to the hospital, Cole."

He let her lead him. They came into the brick building and down the corridor to the kitchen, and here they found Ma Hibbard hobbling about in nightgown and wrapper.

The old woman took a look at them and said, "I've got coffee on." She pulled a chair out from the table and nodded at Manning. "Sit down, son. You're Flint's boy, of course. Land sakes, nobody ever thinks to introduce me to anyone."

Manning seated himself. He needed sleep; he was in a woolly world where nothing much seemed to matter. He stared at the coffee that was set before him; he stirred it for a long time and then slowly sipped it. It was hot and strong and good to taste. It made him feel better. He saw dawn at the window and heard the myriad noises of the hospital. Somebody tiptoed ponderously in and spoke to Laura and tiptoed out. Burke Griffin. Ma Hibbard filled Manning's coffee cup again.

Laura said, "There's an empty bed down the hall, Cole. You'd better sleep awhile."

"Sure," he said and let her lead him to the room. He stretched out on the bed. He didn't try removing his boots, but he felt Laura tug at them. She'd done that at the dugout. Was that yesterday morning or the day before? He'd ridden a lot of miles and had a lot of

267

things crowded at him. Too many. He guessed Laura must be tired, too, and Doc Brownlee and old Packrat — He slept.

He judged that it was past noon when he arose. He got into his boots and rubbed his hand across his jaw. Felt rougher than the bristles of a currying-brush. Now, when the hell had he shaved last? He came along the corridor and found Brownlee's office door open and walked inside. Brownlee was here, working on a patient who was seated on a chair, that hard-jawed Slash 7 hand who'd stopped Brownlee's first bullet when Brownlee had fired through the dugout door. The fellow gave Manning an unblinking stare, saying nothing.

"Good afternoon, Cole," Brownlee said, his fingers busy. "This man tells me that the rest of Slash 7's crew has ridden out, but he was afraid to take the trail without getting patched up first. Figured that jail wouldn't be as bad as blood poisoning. But Burke doesn't want him. Burke says good riddance to the whole bunch."

"It's Griffin's choice," Manning conceded.

Brownlee finished with his work and stood back to admire it. "There," he said to his patient. "You'll have to favor that shoulder for a while, but you'll live."

The man started worming into the remnants of a discarded shirt, but Brownlee had to help him. The man said, "Haven't got a cent on me, Doc. Torgin owed us some pay, but I guess there'll be no collecting it now."

"Forget it," Brownlee said, and when the patient had gone his silent way, Brownlee smiled at Manning. "I put the bullet in him; I suppose it was up to me to dig it out. It's the second charity job I've done for Slash 7 in two days. Found a fellow out there yesterday morning with a bump on his head."

"Gal," Manning said. He'd almost forgotten about Gal. He looked through the window. "Here come Laura and Griffin."

The two entered the hospital and came into the office. Laura was wearing a gingham dress and looked like maybe she'd snatched a few hours' sleep. Ma Hibbard came hobbling down the hallway. She maneuvered into the office and turned to Manning. "You're hungry, I suppose," Ma said. "I could get you something to eat."

"Never mind," Manning said.

Laura asked, "How do you feel, Cole?"

"Fine," he said, though it wasn't so.

Burke Griffin lowered himself to the chair the Slash 7 hand had vacated; Griffin sighed a wheezy sigh. "Sure been stirring my stumps," he said. "But we've got Torgin and Ruxton both boxed up and ready for burying." He shook his head at Manning. "You did a damn-fool thing, son, rushing that door with the two of them planted there, guns in fists. But for luck, you'd be a dead one now and boxed up yourself. But you were thinking of the rest of us, I reckon."

"Something like that," Manning said.

No one spoke then, and strong in Manning was a consciousness that all this talk had been small and of no account, something flung out to keep away from the real thing, the thing which must be said.

"Looks like we're right back where we were before Torgin showed up last night," Dr. Brownlee observed. "Your first case is closed, Cole. All you've got to do is make your report. I'm asking you to leave Flint's name out of it. After all, I'm the one who robbed the stage.

That's all the law needs to know."

"The jewelry can go back to Wells Fargo any time," Griffin said. "And I've released Purdy. In my book, he was the innocent bystander."

"Simple as that, eh?" Manning said. "Don't you folks see? I have to make the same choice my dad made twenty-four years ago when he found Doc, here, with the loot. And I have to remember that Doc saved our lives last night at the coulee dugout. But there's a lot more to it than that. I've got to think about the very thing Flint Manning thought of — the hundreds of lives that a hospital saves."

"You aren't arresting Gramp?" Laura asked.

"I don't know," Manning said. "I don't know — "

Ma Hibbard fixed a stern eye upon him. "You arrest Doc, young man, and I'll stand up in court and swear I robbed that stage myself. I might have done it, too. My legs weren't bad then. And I'd have spent my life in a wheel chair if it hadn't been for Doc Brownlee."

"Who'd believe a woman was the phantom?" Burke Griffin snorted. "But you give me an idea! Folks would likely listen if I testified *I* was the robber. A deputy's pay was slim, and I needed money. How does that sound?" His eyes grew wistful. "I could have been the man, at that. Had a trim figure in those days. Best buck-and-wing dancer in these parts."

Manning thought of the letter Flint Manning had written. A fine time Ma Hibbard or Griffin would have sacrificing themselves if that letter were shown to a court. Had anyone thought to sneak the letter away from him while he slept? He slipped his fingers inside his shirt and touched the pages.

"I'll have to be riding soon," he said. "I've got to make some sort of report to Senator Tom Flowers. You can understand that."

Griffin said, "I took your horse over to the livery. Last time I looked in, she seemed fine and frisky."

Manning said, "I've got to do some thinking."

He walked out to the street. Sunlight drenched Mannington, the shouldering hills standing clear and close, and the mountain air was like wine. He walked along slowly, aimlessly, having no destination; but when he came up the other side of the street and found himself abreast of a restaurant, he turned inside. He got a table by the window and looked at the pencil-scrawled menu and ordered. From here he could see the door of the hospital. Griffin came waddling out and crossed the street toward the jail building.

The waitress placed food before Manning. He began eating. Packrat Purdy came along the street; he spied Manning and said through the screen door, "Howdy, Flint," grinning vacuously. Packrat's addled mind had slipped a cog again. The secret would be forever safe with Packrat, Manning decided, remembering the man's stubbornness and courage in the coulee dugout.

Laura came from the hospital. She must have been watching the street from Brownlee's office window, for she cut directly across to the restaurant and paused in the doorway, her eyes lighting as she spied him. Manning had almost finished eating, but he nodded to the chair opposite. "Hungry?" he asked.

"I'll just watch," she said and seated herself across from him.

He finished his meal. He would have

to go back out to that coulee dugout and pick up his Winchester, he reflected, but he could ride on out of the Bootjack from there. He supposed that Laura would be going to the upper basin again to fetch in the wagon and team, but he'd taken his last ride with her. He knew that now. He had reached his decision, but there was mighty small comfort in it.

He shoved back his coffee cup and his plate. "All through," he said.

She propped her elbows on the edge of the table and cupped her chin in her hands. "What about Gal?" she asked.

"I'd guess that he's ridden out with the rest of Slash 7's crew," he said. "But even if he hasn't, I can't go after him." He'd found the words now to tie to that idea that had been so nebulous when he'd wanted to give Ruxton a chance this morning. "Don't you see? I can't be a part-time lawman, letting one man go but chasing another. It's whole hog or none. That's why I wouldn't have shot Ruxton if he hadn't forced me."

"I see. You've decided not to arrest Gramp, so you can't in clear conscience arrest Gal, either."

"Closed case," he said.

"And where does that leave you, Cole?"

He shrugged. "Right back where I started." He smiled at her; he was remembering his first day in the basin and that ruffed grouse that had put on a frantic act on the slope trail, trying to divert attention from its loved ones. Laura had been like that bird; she'd sprung Purdy from jail and taken him on a wild wagon ride because she'd wanted to spare old Doc Brownlee. And at the head of the canyon trail on another day he had guessed that whatever motivated her was made of some trait admirable and selfless. He felt humble now, looking at her; but there was one thing that remained unchanged for him.

"You see," he said, "you were right about my wanting to stand higher than Flint Manning. Once he'd failed, so that made a chance for me. Only he didn't really fail; I know that now. As it turned out, he proved himself bigger even than the badge he wore. There will be no topping him now, ever."

She said, "You had a big choice to make, too. Today."

"But it was a second choice," he said. "Flint had already made it. And he had

275

less reason to let Doc Brownlee go free."

"Less reason, Cole?"

"Yes," he said. "There was no one like you mixed into it for him."

He stood up then and came around the table and bent over her. She let her hands fall to her lap and looked up at him with her lips slightly parted. He had known her to be a pretty girl the first time he'd got a close look at her; she was never so pretty as now. He cupped her face in his hands and bent and kissed her, not caring who looked on. "Good-by, Laura," he said.

"Cole!" she cried. "Is it because you can't stay? Because the Bootjack would always remind you of failure?"

"Something like that," he said.

"Then I'll come to the Marias!"

"You'd bring the Bootjack with you," he said and walked from the restaurant.

He thought she called after him, but he didn't turn back. He went to the livery and got his horse and saddled up. He climbed to the leather and neck-reined out of the livery and along the street. No need for good-bys; he had made his own strange peace with each of them who'd become close to him. He was taking, he supposed, his last look at Mannington; and as he passed the brick hospital, it seemed to him the biggest thing in the world. No, not quite. The biggest thing was that statue of Flint Manning anchoring the end of the street.

Chapter Seventeen

THE MAN WHO WAITED

The fire, replenished many times, had at last died low in the big living-room of Senator Tom Flowers. Cole Manning's voice trailed off, his tale finished; and in the silence, broken only by the hissing of the gaselier, he sat staring into the embers, a man busy with his thoughts, a man thinking of the law and the limitations of the law and of the things that were bigger than the law could ever be. He felt cramped and sluggish; he felt as though he'd been indoors too long.

"That's all of it," he said.

He picked his empty whisky glass from the marble-topped table, and Flowers made a motion toward the sideboard, but Manning shook his head. What little he'd drunk lay heavy in his stomach. He looked at Flowers. He remembered that he'd gauged Tom Flowers to be two men; and now he'd put himself at the mercy of both, the politician and the ex-cattleman, the man of today, the man of yesterday.

Flowers had made a good listener, not

asking many questions but just sitting, mostly, sometimes nodding his head. Now Flowers lifted Flint Manning's letter from the table where Cole Manning had laid it. He fingered the letter silently and let it drop, and then he began pacing, limping as he went.

"So that was it," he, said softly. "And to think that I was right there in the old days and never suspected the truth! Doc's inheritance was stage loot."

"Now you know," Manning said. He looked at Flowers sharply. "But don't forget, this is off the record; you said so yourself. I'm wondering what your judgment would have been if you'd stood in my boots in Mannington."

Flowers's to-and-fro movement brought him back to the table. He picked up the badge Manning had discarded, the shield-shaped badge of a deputy federal marshal. He held the badge in his hand for a moment, studying it, letting the gaslight play on it, his old face reflective yet unreadable. Then he bent and pinned the badge upon Manning's vest.

"Keep it," Flowers said. "You'll want to resign to the proper authorities, of course. Your life is up along the Marias,

I know, and the Bootjack job is done. But in my house, that badge belongs on you."

Manning said, "You must have got it straight by now. I failed."

Flowers shook his head. "Son, you accused me of having my doubts about you, even though I got your appointment. You were right about that. Any man with a reasonable amount of guts and gun-savvy can be a lawman, but it took a Flint Manning to see that sometimes the law of the statute books falls short of true justice. We'll tell the papers that all you proved in the Bootjack was that Purdy was innocent. They may shout about your failure. Let them. You and I and the several others who count will always know that you didn't fail. As for Torgin and Ruxton, they were killed while attempting armed robbery. And you needn't be concerned about letting Gal slip away. He was the state's problem, not yours."

Manning said, "Damn it, Senator, I didn't come here to get whitewashed!"

"I know," Flowers said. "I'm merely listing the facts of the case."

"Then you're overlooking the most important one. Doc Brownlee robbed a stage and walked free. First because Flint Manning let him go, and again because I made Flint's choice a second time. But Brownlee was a robber, just the same. How do you square that with your conscience, Senator?"

Flowers said, "I deal with the law, too, remember. My job is to have a hand in the making of the law. I long ago learned that no law can be made so tight as to carry full justice for all concerned. That's why we have sheriffs and judges and juries, to make the special application in the special case. Isn't Brownlee's such a case? There is no way of returning that loot, even if Doc had it — which he hasn't. His paying patients hardly meet the overhead. I know, because his hospital has been one of my pet charities across the years. But have you asked yourself one thing? Why did Doc pick that particular stage-coach to rob?"

"Because he must have learned it was carrying that mining syndicate's payroll."

"Precisely. But go a step further in your thinking. The letter Flint Manning wrote referred to the syndicate as one with a reputation for double-dealing.

That outfit was so graft-ridden that it finally split open like a rotten melon. When it did, the stench of it reached all the way to Washington, and some of the syndicate bigwigs are still sitting in jail. Doc knew that outfit was a bigger robber than he could ever be, and Flint knew its reputation, too. That was a factor in Flint's decision, I'm sure. Good out of evil. The special application in the special case."

Manning shook his head. "Some hold-up men to go to stony lonesome, some to walk free? How's a man to know when the law can be turned inside out?"

Flowers said, "When he judges the act of the heart rather than the act of the hand. Let's put this case to a test. Earlier this evening, I remarked that it was just plain luck that brought the old case to life again. But what did that stroke of luck represent to each one it affected? To Torgin it was a possible chance for blackmail; to Ruxton it meant a quick dollar of bounty money. Laura saw it as a means of relieving her grandfather of a worry which she herself didn't rightly understand. Burke Griffin and Ma Hibbard were of a mind to protect a kindly old doctor whom they both loved dearly. To Gal it was an opportunity to take out his twisted hate on the son of Flint Manning. To you it was a chance to throw a bigger shadow than your father. The motive of each showed his worth or lack of worth. Yours wasn't a good motive when you first hit the Bootjack, son. Laura recognized the unworthiness that drove you and tried to tell you so. But in the end you proved as big as Flint Manning because you made a choice as sound as his."

"But it was a second choice."

"We stray from the point," Flowers said. "What of the motives of Doc Brownlee before and after? Once that robbery meant to him a chance to do a great good. But when the old case came to life again, he saw a means of atonement for whatever taint of evil his original act held. It's on that basis that you've got to judge Doc Brownlee."

Manning smiled faintly. "And so Brownlee stays free, eh? And you believe that he deserves to stay free."

Flowers became a stern man in the gaslight. "I am a politician, son.. I try to be an honest one. If Brownlee's motives, past and present, had held the least taint of selfishness, I would insist that you go back to the Bootjack and bring him in. I would order his arrest, no matter how much it hurt me to do so. Instead, I have given you back your badge. You see, Doc has paid his pound of flesh, and more. If Flint Manning had arrested him that long-ago night, the law would probably have sent Doc to Deer Lodge for twenty years. Flint let him go, so Doc sentenced himself to life. Not at making saddles behind bars or tending to a warden's flower garden but at serving the people of Bootjack Basin. Twenty years and more he's been in that hospital, and there he'll stay till the day he dies. A parole board consists of a very few people. Didn't Burke Griffin offer to parole him? Didn't Ma Hibbard? In fact, they went further than a parole aboard. They showed a willingness to finish out his sentence for him, not the one he imposed on himself but the one the law might have imposed."

Manning said slowly, "I never thought about it that way."

Flowers fell to pacing with that peculiar limp again. "This old leg's giving me trouble," he remarked. "I'll have to get down to Mannington one of these days and let Brownlee have another look at it. He's one of the few doctors in the country I'd trust. When I got that bullet, most medicos would have had to saw off my leg. Brownlee saved it for me. I owe him a very great deal."

"You, too!" Manning said.

"Sure as shootin'," Flowers declared, his round, cherubic face bland. "I'm mighty glad you didn't arrest Doc. What would Washington have said when the Gentleman from Montana got up in court and swore he was the one who stopped that stagecoach twenty-four years ago? Ma Hibbard and Burke Griffin couldn't have lied worth a whoop on the stand, but I'll bet I'd have made it stick!"

He walked to the marble-topped table and lifted Flint Manning's letter. He thumbed through it, reading a snatch here and there; and then he limped to the fireplace and dropped the letter into its maw and watched the paper catch and burn. He faced about then.

"The case is closed," he said.

Manning stood up and picked his sombrero from the able. "I've got a bed waiting for me."

Flowers said, "I think there is one last piece of unfinished business. You, son. You and your need to stand bigger than Flint Manning. Can't you be content with having stood as big?"

"It's not that," Manning said. "I'm partly straightened out in my mind. Laura hit the nail on the head, and you clinched it tonight. Trouble is, I never had a father, not a flesh-and-blood one. I was sired by a legend, and I've been expected to live up to that legend ever since. I thought that the old case would give me a chance to make myself into a legend, too. But that wouldn't have been what I was looking for. I know that now."

Flowers's face softened. "Whatever you seek, may you find it. Whatever trail you take, may it lead you to peace with yourself." He extended his hand. "Good night, son." He ushered Manning to the door and closed it behind him.

The porch was no longer peopled with ghostly faces and alive with ghostly voices, Manning reflected; he had rid himself of them by his talk with Flowers; he had laid all the ghosts but one, the big-beaked, stern-eyed one that was made of a statue's bronze. He gave his

286

belt a hitch and reminded himself that he must leave his gun in his hotel room if he did any more sashaying around Helena. He came down the steps and started along the street toward the Bristol.

Must be about two in the morning, he judged. Maybe three. Birds were making fretful, sleepy sounds in the trees; leaves stirred to the faintest of breezes. He remembered how the birds had sounded that last morning in Mannington. He quickened his pace. A good chunk of distance lay between here and Main Street, and Manning strode along steadily. What a heap of jawing he'd done tonight! He kept turning the talk over in his mind, and he found some balm in it; he would never have to face himself before the bar of conscience as far as Doc Brownlee was concerned. He had the wisdom of Tom Flowers to thank for that, and the consolation of knowing that his own instinct had been right. Closed case.

He was nearly to the slant of State Street now, and the stars in the east were beginning to fade. Later than he thought. He came abreast of a big red brick building and was reminded of

Brownlee's charity hospital. He wondered then if all brick buildings would forever re mind him of the hospital and thus recollected his fear of the early evening, that the Marias would have lost it wild charm, with nothing looking the same again. But that fear was a laid ghost, too. He put his hand out to the building and felt its solidness.

Another block or so to the Bristol. Thus thinking, he was a tired man, and unwary, with no full consciousness of the man who stepped from the shadow of the brick building until he was face to face with the fellow. He knew that tall shape before he heard and recognized the voice. For an instant there was no reality to this. Here was a finished thing showing a last unfinished edge. For Gal was standing before him, his teeth a white flash in the darkness.

Gal said, "I've been behind you all the way from the Bootjack. I was close on your heels tonight, but not close enough. I found your name on the Bristol register, and I've waited half the night for you to head back there. This is the end of it. Bring out your gun blazing this time. We'll finish here and now."

Chapter Eighteen

FADING HOOFBEATS

He wanted no gun fight with Gal. He had long regretted cheating Gal that night he'd clouted the man before Slash 7's root cellar so that Laura might be freed, and Laura had convinced him even then of the senselessness of fighting Gal. He had since faced up to Mack Torgin and Slade Ruxton and known the aftermath of killing and found no taste for it, and he'd been done with gunplay then, done for all time. Or so he'd thought. But here stood Gal with a challenge flung out and no choice about it, and Gal was backing away from him and drawing at the same time. Manning got his own gun out and brought it up and gave Gal the only answer that could be made.

The sense of unreality was still strong in Manning; he stood apart from what was happening, viewing it with rapt wonder. He saw Gal's gun clear leather and come up, and he sensed that his own draw was faster than Gal's. He felt his forty-five beat back against his palm, and the roar was great in his ears. But in the last instant before he pulled the trigger, he had time for re-membering that Gal had balked at tor-turing Packrat Purdy; he had time for pity. And so he moved his gun barrel slightly to the left.

Gal seemed to shudder and turn half about, his face a white, stricken smear against the darkness. Gal's gun slipped from his fingers and dropped with a clatter. Manning took long steps toward Gal and kicked the gun aside. Gal said through clenched teeth, "I think you've broken my arm."

Manning said, "Let's have a look at it."

"Get away from me," Gal said and shrank against the building. "I want nothing from you."

Somewhere near by windows were banging open and sleepy voices calling, and Manning was reminded again of the Bootjack and the night his gun and Torgin's and Ruxton's had aroused a town. He paid no heed to the voices. He said, "Don't be a fool, Gal. The fight's over and done with. You don't want to stand there bleeding to death."

Gal's face was a haggard mask in which those blue eyes blazed. "All those years in stony lonesome," he muttered.

"They slowed me down — They slowed me down. Once I'd have been able to give anyone with your speed an edge and still split his heart before he could ear back the hammer. My speed is just one more thing a Manning took away from me."

Manning said, "I wish I could take away your hate." He came close to Gal and reached out and felt of Gal's arm, being gentle about this. "I don't think the bone is broken," Manning said. He whipped off his bandanna and wadded it and handed it to Gal. "Here, hold this against the wound."

Feet pounded along the walk. Someone drawn by the shot, Manning thought. A blue-uniformed figure shaped up, night stick swinging. "What's going on here?" demanded a voice with a touch of brogue to it.

"Nothing to worry about, officer," Manning said. "You've got someone here who needs a doctor, though." He remembered the decision he'd made about Gal in Mannington and felt a last regret. "You'll find you've bagged a prize. This man is an escaped convict from Deer Lodge. He's down on the books as Joe Bridger."

"We've checked a hundred freight trains, looking for him," the policeman said. "And just who would you be?"

Manning touched his badge.

"I'll take him along," the policeman said. "He looks able to walk." He moved close to Gal and began to run his hands over the man.

"You needn't worry," Gal said, but it was to Manning that he spoke. "I left my hide-out gun in Slash 7's yard the night you clouted me. It was no damn thing for a man to be carrying, anyway."

The policeman finished his search. He looked at Manning. "You can make your report on him tonight or tomorrow, whichever you're so minded, Marshal."

Manning said, "Deer Lodge will tell you all you need to know. If I'm wanted, I'm staying at the Bristol tonight. To-morrow I ride out."

"Come along, you," the policeman said and took Gal's good arm. He bent and picked up Gal's fallen gun and stowed it away.

Manning said, "So long, Gal."

Gal showed him his teeth. "The hell with you!"

Manning said, "Just a minute," a memory stirring him. "What was the rest of it you were going to tell me that night by the root cellar? Remember? You said there was more to it than I knew. I was to be told when my gun was loaded."

Gal said, "It wouldn't matter to you. But the plain truth is that I didn't do it, Manning."

"Didn't do what?"

"That killing up on the Marias eighteen years ago. They gave me life for it, but I didn't do it. Flint Manning made a mistake, bringing me in."

The policeman laughed. "They're all innocent when they're caught, every mother's son of them."

But Manning was looking hard at Gal. "Are you sure?" Manning demanded, and excitement stirred deep in his stomach.

"I was riding with some fast and loose boys in those days, Manning. Everybody up there knew it. When Flint Manning cut sign after that killing, he got sniffing along the wrong trail. I happened to be at the end of it. When I tried to tell the straight story in the courtroom, the very fact that the great Flint Manning had brought me in was proof enough to the jury that I must be the jigger they wanted. You couldn't make them believe that Flint Manning could possibly have made a mistake. So they threw the book at me."

"Are you saying that Flint perjured himself?"

Gal shook his head. "Probably he thought he had the right man. But he was wrong, dead wrong."

"Could you prove it now?"

Gal shrugged. "Given time enough, and the chance. I used to read the Shelby paper in prison. A few old-timers are left up there. If I could get some of them to put two and two together, they might come up with the right answer."

"Then why didn't you head for the Marias after you walked away from Deer Lodge?"

Gal's face turned cold with the old hatred. "Because I wanted to square up for the eighteen years I shouldn't have put in behind bars. Because the Mannings owed me for those eighteen years, and I wanted to collect. Can you savvy that?"

"Yes," Manning said. "I can understand. And I'll speak for you, if you're telling the truth."

"The hell with you," Gal said again. "I don't want your stinking pity or your help. I just wanted you to know what Flint Manning did to me."

The policeman tugged at Gal. "Come along, now. 'Tis fever talk you're babbling."

Manning watched the two of them move on down the slope. He stood there in the night, his mind full of what he'd been told, his mind groping, for somewhere in Gal's talk there had been a significance greater than Gal realized. Manning shook his head, wanting mightily to flush out of chaotic thinking the thing that eluded him. He was tired, he guessed, tired from the long trail up from the Bootjack, tired from the long hours in Tom Flowers's parlor. He came on down the slope to the Bristol and got his key from the clerk. It was a different clerk from the one who'd registered him. He climbed to his room and let himself in and seated himself on the edge of the bed.

He should sleep, he knew, but he didn't feel like sleeping. He sat here and stared hard at the design in the carpet, not really seeing it, and slowly realized what he must do. He would check into that wild story of Gal's and find if it held a shred of truth. He would talk to the old-timers along the Marias; and then, if need be, he would throw weight to make Gal a free man. He would take the matter up with Senator Flowers; he would go and see the governor and the warden at Deer Lodge and the parole board. He would do this because Gal was a man worth salvaging.

No, Gal was only part of the reason; and now he knew fully why he must right a wrong. He thought long about it; and then, on impulse, he went downstairs and stepped out of the Bristol. He was surprised to see dawn showing. He crossed over to the police station, which stood near the head of Main. He came in and found a sleepy desk sergeant on duty. He identified himself and made an inquiry and was ushered to the door of a cell in which Gal sat, his arm in a sling.

Gal said, "Did you have to make sure they got me locked up?"

Manning looked at him through the bars. "I want you to know I meant what I said about speaking for you. I'll do more than that. I'll get you paroled or pardoned. Will you help me?"

Gal said, "You've got no reason to do anything for me."

"I'll prove you're wrong about that," Manning said. "And when we've squared you with the law, I'll have a job waiting for you on my Marias ranch. Maybe it isn't much of a deal, but I'd like to try giving you eighteen good years for those eighteen bad ones."

Gal said, "Talk comes mighty cheap," but his surety sounded shaken.

Manning said, "I'll start working on your case as soon as I've got some sleep. But I wanted to tell you first. Later I'll be back to go over the details with you. Is there anything you need meanwhile?"

Gal hesitated; his face worked, showing how hard-dying his old thinking was. Then: "I left my cayuse at the livery stable across the gulch. I'd like to be sure he gets good care."

Manning said, "He'll get the best."

"Thanks," Gal said. His face was puzzled. "Just what's your stake?"

"A last ghost laid," Manning said, but he guessed that made no sense to Gal.

He turned and walked out of the police station and stood on the street with the hills crowding close about. He knew now what he'd been trying to put into words when he'd told Tom Flowers, "Trouble is, I never had a father, not a flesh-and-blood one. I was sired by a legend."

That was it. Every boy had rights that had been denied him. He had clutched tight his few memories of a father telling his son about Virginia City, a man riding with his boy behind his saddle to take a holiday and look for Indian arrowheads, a man leading his boy down a street to perch him on the desk in the jail building. He had cherished those remembrances of a human Flint Manning; but pitted against them always was the legend, the oft-told tales of an invincible one who had never failed save once. And not really then. But at last he'd grasped the full significance that had escaped him when Gal had spoken of an error made. He'd learned from Gal that Flint Manning had been human — human enough to have made a mistake. And now he could rectify that mistake and so be son to his father. Not to top Flint Manning, as he'd once hoped, but to stand as kin to him, blood of his blood, human and frail.

And so the ghostly hoofbeats faded out forever for Cole Manning, the last haunting murmur dying away. For he understood now that always there had been for him a special kind of ghostly hoofbeats ringing in his ears, not those made by a phantom holdup man riding in the Bootjack, but the hoofbeats of one who had ridden sure and invincible and had thereby ceased to be a man, had become instead a legend and a statue — beyond a boy's reach. And in the first of this morning, Cole Manning listened to the hush and stood at last close to his father.

He stretched his arms and felt ready for anything. Let those reporters come knocking at his door; he would have a story for them, though not the one they expected. The power of the press could help Gal.

A feeling of well-being built in him, so great that it must be shared. He knew who would listen and understand, but she was far away, down there in the Bootjack, lost to him once, but waiting. He would go to her when this last chore was done; he would present to her his achievement; and she would share the glory of it, and the understanding. So thinking, he crossed over toward the hotel, walking high and proud.

We hope you have enjoyed this Large Print book. Other Thorndike Press or Chivers Press Large Print books are available at your library or directly from the publishers.

For more information about current and upcoming titles, please call or write, without obligation, to:

Thorndike Press
P.O. Box 159
Thorndike, Maine 04986
USA
Tel. (800) 223-2336

OR

Chivers Press Limited
Windsor Bridge Road
Bath BA2 3AX
England
Tel. (0225) 335336

All our Large Print titles are designed for easy reading, and all our books are made to last.